A CAT
CALLED AMNESIA

'I have a strong h
turn out to be ver
death problem for

The stray cat had t
Bleeker's holiday farmhouse during a thunderstorm. Not that 'Amnesia' was just any old stray cat, but a magnificent one, well-fed and beautifully marked. The Bleeker children began a desperate search to find his owner before the end of the holidays, but every clue proved useless. It wasn't until they saw the strange behaviour of the 'caravan lady' that they thought they were about to solve the whole mystery at last.

E.W. Hildick has won the Hans Christian Andersen Award, and his children's books are popular throughout the world. A CAT CALLED AMNESIA is based on fact: the Hildick's own cat, Butter, having come to them in exactly the same mysterious way. Unlike the Bleekers, though, the Hildick's still have not discovered where Butter came from . . .

Jacket illustration by Val Biro

ABOUT THE AUTHOR

E. W. Hildick is the author of over forty books for children and teenagers, including the *Louie* books and the *McGurk* stories. Among his children's books are two famous Louie stories, *Louie's S.O.S.* and *Louie's Lot*, which won the Hans Christian Andersen Award for the best children's book of the year. E. W. Hildick's books have been translated into French, Danish, Dutch, Spanish, Russian, Yugoslavian and Icelandic.

Before he began writing books, Mr Hildick worked as a journalist. He and his wife now spend their time living both in the States, where his children's books are as successful as they are here, and in Ireland.

E.W. HILDICK

ILLUSTRATED BY VAL BIRO

A CAT CALLED AMNESIA

KNIGHT BOOKS
Hodder and Stoughton

First published 1977 by André Deutsch

Knight Books edition 1978

The characters in this book are entirely imaginary and bear no relation to any real person.

Printed and bound in Great Britain for Hodder and Stoughton Paperbacks, a division of Hodder and Stoughton Ltd., Mill Road, Dunton Green, Sevenoaks, Kent (Editorial Office: 47 Bedford Square, London, WC1 3DP) by Richard Clay (The Chaucer Press), Ltd., Bungay, Suffolk

ISBN 0 340 23249 8

Contents

1. A Life or Death Problem 1
2. The Farmhouse 7
3. The Storm 14
4. The Cat's Description (Physical) 21
5. Search Report–First Day–First Inquiry 25
6. Search Report–First Day–Second and Third Inquiries 31
7. Search Report–Second Day 40
8. The New Deal 48
9. The Cat Comes In 56
10. Amnesia? 65
11. The Truck and the Table 79
12. News of a Home 91
13. The Mystery of the Doors 99
14. The Cat and the Woman 108
15. The Split 115
16. Stake-Out 123
17. The Final Clue 135
18. The Final Report 143

To
Mona and Dave,
Ann, David, Sam, and Adam
also
Tarzan, Jane, Priscilla, Charles,
and all the other cats
(not forgetting the Wallaces)
who've made our many returns so very happy
up at the farm and at Port Washington

1

A LIFE OR DEATH PROBLEM

"I warned you. I told you what would happen. You two girls particularly. Feed a stray cat and he'll hang around. Pet a stray cat and he'll never leave. So all right then. That's what has happened. Right after supper I'll call the ASPCA."

That was my father speaking. Mr. Clyde Bleeker. He is a tall man with sandy hair, a thin face, and thick glasses.

To hear his words and the tone of his voice you would think he was back home. In his den. Sitting up in the black judge's chair behind his desk and being very stern, with all of us kids standing in front of it and looking down at our shoes.

But no.

This was out in the open. On the grass in front of the porch up at the farm. He was dressed in his shorts and a loose shirt, and he had a towel over his shoulder still wet from after his swim. Dressed like that, at a time like that, he should have been relaxed and happy and joking with his children. He wasn't, though. After all, he was right. He *had* warned us.

"Oh, but Daddy, they—they'll put him to sleep, poor old cat!"

My sister Trina. Age twelve. Sitting on the porch step, looking up from the latest book she was reading, blinking. She should wear glasses, too, but she keeps breaking them or losing them, so you might as well forget them. Her hair is dark brown, like Mom's and mine. She has a habit of clutching it and pulling it when she is anxious. She was clutching it and pulling it now, when she said that about the ASPCA putting the cat to sleep.

My father frowned harder.

"Possibly. Possibly not. But we just have no choice in the matter. *We* can't take him in."

"But we can, Daddy, we can. He likes it here. He loves it."

This was my other sister, Katie. She's seven. Also sitting on the porch step, hugging the cat himself and brushing her cheek against his big round soft furry head. I don't think she quite got that bit my father said. About possibly putting the cat to sleep. Otherwise she'd have hollered those words, not murmured them. But she's a dreamy sort of girl. Never listens to half of what people say. She has sandy hair like Dad's, but thicker and shinier. She is just a bit fat still and she has two big new front teeth.

Katie is Dad's favourite, I think. Anyway, his frown softened when he answered her:

"*Obviously* he loves it here. Sure. No argument there,

honey. But we happen to be here on vacation only. And then what? We can't take him back home with us. Back to the apartment. Even if I—uh—we wanted. Animals are just not allowed in the building. You know that. And we can't abandon him here. That would be cruel."

"Sir, may I say something?"

My brother Ray, thirteen. Boss man. Don't be fooled by that polite request. If Ray wants to say something he'll say it no matter what. But he likes to *sound* polite. It makes him feel grown-up. He's tall and skinny and he too has sandy hair, which he grows long and sort of bushy and curly.

"Sure. Go ahead."

"I agree with you, Father. It *is* the girls' fault—"

"It is *not* then!"

Katie. Louder now. So that the cat's ears go back and he wriggles some.

"Be quiet, Katie. Go on, Ray."

"I was just going to say—"

Pause while he scratches around under the plaster cast, just above the left wrist, where he broke it at school the week before we came to the farm. Although it keeps him from swimming and even makes it hard for him to hold a camera steady, which is his other big hobby, he's getting quite smart with that plaster cast. Makes the most of it, I mean. Attracting attention, sympathy. Things like that. Like now.

"I was going to say that although it *was* the girls' fault, why be so quick to call the ASPCA? I mean we haven't really tried yet, have we? I mean why not give us another day, two days, to track down its true owners?"

"Oh, yes, Daddy! We could really concentrate. Like

in a detective story. Missing Persons Bureau. Only the other way around. Missing *Homes* Bureau."

That was Trina again. Book forgotten.

"Yes, yes, *yes*! Say yes!"

Katie. *Very* loud this time. So loud that:

"Ngraaaow!"

Yes. The cat himself joined in. That was he his very own self, the cause of all the trouble.

Maybe it was that interruption that did it. Made my father change his mind like this:

"Well . . . all right. Two days then. Two more days and no more. Six P.M., Wednesday, OK?. . . . But if you haven't traced his owners by then, I call the ASPCA and that's final."

The only members of the family who didn't join in that discussion were Mom and me. Mom was in the kitchen fixing supper, so that takes care of her. As for me, well, yes, I *was* out there with the others but I was too busy tape recording all they were saying to say anything myself. You see, I sensed this would develop into something big. Something about the vacation that would be worth recording.

I'm Angus. Age eleven. They call me The Recording Angus because of my hobby. Like The Recording *Angel*, get it? I got the recorder for my tenth birthday from my Uncle Charles. It was a used one even then, but it works fine, as you can hear. Normally I don't bother to do all that fancy splicing—cutting up the tape and sticking in bits of my own explanations between other people's speeches. But as I say, I have a strong hunch that this cat business will turn out to be very special, and maybe one day, when the record is complete, it can all be copied down for other people to share. I would like that.

Anyway, let me give you more of the background, more about the cat and how he came to us two days ago and started this life or death problem for us to solve.

Oh, yes!

"Life or death" is right. Because if we *do* solve it, the cat will live. And if we *don't* solve it, and the ASPCA can't find a home for it, the cat will surely die.

2

THE FARMHOUSE

The apartment where we normally live is back in Philadelphia. It is in a new high-rise building near the Penn Centre there.

The farmhouse where we are staying on vacation is up here in Connecticut. It is not far from the big river itself and near a small creek that runs into it.

Now, what Dad said about no animals back home is quite true. My friend Terry Hart who lives in the same building tried to keep a tortoise in his bedroom. But when the super found out, there was a terrible row and the Harts nearly had to move because of it. The tortoise had to go to a cousin of his out near Harrisburg. Imagine! An iddy-bitty tortoise not being allowed!

Anyway, because of the no-animals rule back home, that was one reason why we looked forward especially to coming here. I mean "farmhouse," "farm"—the very words. What would they be without animals?

Well, I'll tell you.

They would be like this place.

Because it is not a working farmhouse any more. It is now used strictly for vacations. My father and two of our uncles bought it last year and the three families take turns using it. (Except Thanksgiving, when we're *all* going to be here.)

Don't get me wrong, though. We like it. It is a very interesting place in many ways. I will now tell you why. I will also splice into my description some of the comments the others made on another tape. (That was when I was making a mere ordinary record of the holiday, like a snapshot album in sound.)

The farmhouse is isolated, for one thing.

"You could think we were hundreds of miles from anywhere else."

"Thousands."

That was my father who spoke first. The glummer voice saying "Thousands" was Ray's. I guess he was wondering where all the girls would be, so far from a city.

But the rest of us thought this was a good thing. Like being pioneers or something. Because to get to it you have to go along a narrow country road. When you come to a rusty mailbox and a gap in the hedge opposite, that is where you turn off onto a still narrower road. This is a dirt road. It winds and rises up at the side of a field and there the farmhouse is, sort of tucked in a fold at the top of the field, with some woods hanging over it on a hillside behind it.

"Very picturesque."

That was Mom.

"Lovely, lovely, lovely! Just like in the story I was reading last week!"

That was Trina.

"Where *are* we?"

That was Katie, who'd been fast asleep for the last twenty miles.

But Mom and Trina were right. All those white boards and the porch and a real chimney. It sure looked good up there, and we younger kids were glad to get out and run the last few hundred yards up through the long whippy grass and the flowers and feel all those stalks brushing cool against our bare legs.

And not just the outside. The inside is interesting also. Bare boards on the floor that make terrific echoes. Old furniture so it doesn't matter if you kick it or fall over it. A room for us boys with two bunks and an old brown picture of President Lincoln. A room for the girls with two bunks and pictures on the walls made out of old dried flowers. A dark deep cellar smelling of earth. An attic with rafters, smelling of apples and dust.

"And talking of smells, what is it I can smell all over the house, Clyde? A faint sweetish smell. Can't you smell it? Oh, I do hope it isn't anything *dead*!"

"Ha! ha! Anything *dead*! You getting this down, Angus? What your mother just said? . . . No, dear. It's the gas you can smell. Propane. Nothing to worry about. Just a good honest country smell."

"Huh! Better than the gasoline fumes back home, anyway."

"You'll soon get used to it."

What my father told my mother there was right. We *have* soon got used to it. And it's a good thing, too, because we depend on that propane for everything. For lighting, for cooking, and even for the old refrigerator in the summer kitchen in back. The gas itself comes from a big cylinder in an outbuilding.

And—talking of outbuildings—no bathroom.

The only water is from a well. We get it up through a big iron pump in the kitchen.

"I pulled it and nothing happened!"

Trina said that.

"Maybe something's stuck up the spout."

That was Ray. Trina bent her head and twisted her neck. Now listen to this next!

"Yerrowch! You—you—"

That's Trina again, her voice lost amongst all that splashing sound as the water gushed all over her face when Dad gave the handle another pump.

"Now maybe you'll all remember. It takes *two* pumps to get it flowing."

(Tina got her own back later, when she pretended she *had* given two pumps and still nothing had happened, and Dad put his head under to look up, and she let him have it. I'm sure sorry I didn't have my tape recorder going that time. But I suppose he'd have censored it anyway, the things he said then.)

But I was saying about no true bathroom, and this is one of the really great things about the farmhouse. All there is for a toilet is an outhouse in back of the main building. It has a plank with two holes, and a door you keep shut by sticking out your feet, and a deep pit underneath the plank, and a sack of lime to throw a shovelful from, over onto what you've done. That lime is instead of water. And it is great, that outhouse. Just great. Even Katie likes using it if it is not at night.

But—

No animals. No *farm* animals, anyway.

A horsebarn, yes, but no horses.

A pony pen, yes, but no ponies.

The only animals are the small wild ones. About

twelve million chipmunks. A groundhog or two. A possum that comes visiting the trash cans in the middle of the night. We sometimes hear him, but we've never seen him yet.

And that's about all, apart from the birds and a black snake that Ray says he's seen.

So you can see. When the cat came two days ago and sort of took us over, it was not only the girls that welcomed him. We boys did too, without making too much of a production of it. Even Mom did, I suspect.

In fact that gives me an idea. Since we have not heard anything from Mom about the cat in this report, I'll just go to her now and see if I can trap her into making a statement. I mean about how she too welcomed the cat. You never know. If we don't find the cat's true home in another two days, as we've promised, we'll need an extension. And if we're going to get an extension, the evidence that Mom herself likes the cat should come in handy.

(By the way, she is small and dark and plump with a clear round face, no wrinkles, a *baby* face. We kid her about this. About how she looks more like Trina's big sister than her mother. She pretends to get mad but she can't help smiling really.)

But now for Mom's evidence. If you hear thumping noises, that is because she's doing things with dough on the kitchen table, real dough I mean, to make our own bread with, which is another of the things we like about this place.

"Mom, I'm making a special report on the cat problem on tape. Tell us, please, what you thought about him when he first showed up."

"Well . . . . Well I could see he had been well cared for. I guess that's the first thing I thought. He wasn't thin. His coat was sleek. He was affectionate. You know. Tame. But he *was* hungry, boy, was he!"

"So you helped to feed him?"

"Well, yes. You know I did. I mean I didn't object when the girls asked for scraps, if that's what you mean. Say, what *is* this?"

"No, just asking. Just for the record, Mom."

"Record, eh? Hmm, well—we'd better get it straight then, hadn't we?"

"Sure, Mom. You go right ahead and—"

"What I mean is that I did *not* regard him as a real stray. He looked too well cared for. OK? I just thought that he'd lost his way temporarily, scared by the storm. I thought as soon as he'd had a meal and a rest he'd be on his way back. Cats are good at that, you know—finding their way home."

"Sure. That's—"

"But if he *is* a real stray, your father is right. We can't *think* of keeping him. He must be turned in. It's hard, I know. But there it is. To encourage him when there's no hope of keeping him would be cruel."

Well, at least I got the evidence I wanted.

So next let me report on the cat's actual arrival, just after the storm Mom mentioned. Let me try to remember every detail.

Because—I'll say it again—you never know.

This problem might prove tougher than we think. Then even the tiniest detail might turn out to be a valuable clue in helping us to trace the cat's true owner.

3

THE STORM

I could kick myself for not recording that storm on Saturday morning. But then it was so terrific I just didn't have time to think.

Besides, it started while I was still asleep.

I dreamed that someone was hammering all around me.

I dreamed that I was going to be shipped someplace, like a monkey to a zoo, in a big crate, and men were hammering the last nails in above my head.

Then it became a half-dream. The crate and the men faded and this time I thought it was happening right there in the room, and that it was Ray above me, going mad with the itching under the plaster on his wrist. I had this half-dream that Ray was thumping his plaster against the edge of the bunk.

Thwack! Thwack! Thwack!

Getting madder and madder.

Thwack-thwack-thwack! *Thwack*! THWACK!

And then it burst. In my half-dream, the plaster burst

and the bits fell in a kind of waterfall, in a *plaster*fall, shuttering and rattling down in a torrent, only never seeming to stop, so that even in my half-dream I couldn't help wondering, thinking Ray's plaster must have been as big as a barn for it to take all that time for the bits to pour down.

Then—just when it slowed to a trickle—more thumps, only louder, and this time not just above me but all around, so that I thought Ray had jumped out of bed and was running around the room on those bare echoing boards in some kind of heavy boots.

Then there was a great, gigantic, *tremendous* flash that got clear through my eyelids and I woke up fully.

"Golly!" I said. "What was *that*?"

"I guess we're in for a storm," said Ray.

His voice came from the bunk above, so I realized I had been dreaming.

Then came a rattling sound at the window, and the rattling became a drumming, and a flash lit up every one of the half million raindrops there, sliding down, bouncing off—and the storm was on.

I'd never—*we'd* never—none of us kids had ever seen anything like it.

I mean in Philly you see some terrific storms there, sure. From twenty-one storeys up you get to see some *glorious* storms, you can imagine. We've watched the lightning flickering around William Penn's statue's head like a nest of snakes in the brim of his hat. We've seen it streaking in all directions down the sky and between other tall buildings. We've seen it bouncing in sheets from one loop of the river to another.

All very spectacular.

But somehow to see sights like that from a comfortable

apartment in the city, even so high up, is not the same. You feel more sealed off from it. It's like watching something on television. The noise seems to be cut down by the walls and the thick double glass. The hum of the air conditioning can still be heard and it puts a fuzzy wrapper over the thunderclaps and tones them down. The flashes and flickers and streaks and sheets of lightning are also toned down, because even when the lights in the apartment are turned off there are still the lights all over the city, sending up their usual glare.

Mind you, we never felt any of this at any time *during* those storms over the city. We used to think that nobody ever could see such storms anyplace else.

But after seeing and hearing and smelling (I swear I smelled sulphur sizzling from time to time) and feeling (I swear I felt a tingling all over my body, also) and even *tasting* (a kind of metal taste)—after seeing, hearing, smelling, feeling, and tasting a storm like last Saturday's, here in the country—*pow*!

The thing is you feel a part of it. The thin walls and the country quietness make the thunder get straight to you. The windows rattle. The rain comes splashing through cracks. The gusts of whipped-up wind come surging up under the floorboards and barrelling down the chimneys.

Then again, because of the normal country darkness, the lightning comes all the clearer and brighter—so clear and bright it leaves pictures on your eyeballs kind of, even when it dies away, and echoes in your eardrums the same. Pictures like the whole of the hill above us, all those trees tossing about like waves, like an angry sea. Or just one twig of one branch of one tree, turned up, in a blaze of gold, beckoning. And echoes that were shrieks as well as thuds and thwacks and rattles, and sometimes sobs, really strange these were, like someone was losing that ninepins game in the sky that people talk about. Like someone was losing and had staked a lot of money on it, even his life maybe, and was wanting out.

Of course all the rest of the family were awake, not just Ray and me. And I guess they all felt the same as I was feeling, even though nobody spoke much. I guess we were all just a little bit scared too, *I* don't mind admitting it, but we were all too interested to go hide in a corner, even if there *was* such a corner where the storm couldn't reach.

One interesting thing was the bathroom set-up. It was the only time we ever wished the bathroom was back inside the house. But it would have been impossible going to the outhouse in all that rain, even if you didn't mind risking sitting where the lightning looked ready to strike at any moment.

That was a minus for the farmhouse, sure enough.

But there was also a big plus. Mom was the first to note it.

"Well at least the utilities are safe," she said. "We don't have a phone to worry about and there are no power lines to be struck down. We have light and we can cook and I might as well fix breakfast now that we're all up."

She was the scaredest of us all, I think, and was glad of the excuse to get busy in the kitchen.

Well, gradually it got light.

And gradually the storm died down.

And by nine o'clock the rain had stopped.

And by 9:15 the sun was out, sparkling in the grass and

on the trees, and we kids were getting ready to go out. We were keen to investigate for damage to the outbuildings (we'd already checked on *the* outhouse, of course, even before the rain had finally stopped) and we were also hoping to find struck trees, blasted in half clear down the middle of their trunks, and major landslides blocking the road, and vast floods, things like that. I mean it had certainly seemed like that sort of a storm. Well, we never did find anything like that, but that is not what I was leading up to, which is this:

Just as we went onto the front porch, getting ready to go in search of disasters, Katie said:

"Oh, what a lovely cat!"

And there he was.

Out in the field at the front, in the long grass.

There was yellow pollen dust blotching his black and grey stripes and a wet purple petal clinging to the fur between his ears. He was staring straight up at us with his wide clear green eyes and he was making those big noiseless cat cries at us, as if he was one fourth scared of us but three fourths mad at us about something—maybe thinking the storm had been all our fault.

"Poor thing!" said Trina. "I wonder if he was out in it all."

Ray said:

"It doesn't look all *that* wet to me. No more than it would get from walking through wet grass. It probably took shelter. Cats aren't dumb. Here, kitty, kitty!"

The cat shrank back.

Ray shrugged.

"Dumb cat!" he said, and lost interest.

Personally, I couldn't blame the cat. Seeing Ray's

plaster cast reaching out toward it, it must have thought this was a club or something.

So *I* said, "Here, kitty, kitty!"—but again the cat shrank back, but I was not all that much interested at the time, so I shrugged too.

But when Katie said, "Here, kitty, kitty!" that was different, and the next we knew it was in her arms, with one of its own long arms around her neck and purring like a speedboat. Just as if it knew that Trina was already gathering scraps for it in the kitchen!

And that was the start of it all, with Mom and Dad not paying much attention at first, being more concerned just then to check for leaks in the roof and things like that.

So he got his first meal. Cold cuts and warm milk.

And now I will describe the cat.

4

THE CAT'S DESCRIPTION

(Physical)

Already I have mentioned several things about this cat. For instance, the following:

1. He is a male cat.
2. He is marked with black and grey stripes.
3. He has green eyes.
4. He is a large cat—fully grown.
5. He is affectionate—
   especially with girls and women.

All right. Now let me add to that list things we have noticed since he first arrived out of that storm.

Like being a neutered cat, which my Dad spotted first.

"What's neutered?" said Katie.

"It means he's been altered," said Trina, without looking up from her book.

"Altered how?" asked Katie. "Altered like a dress is altered?"

"Exactly," said Ray. "He's had pieces snipped off here and there."

"Where?"

"So he can't have kittens with a girl cat," said Mom. "Now eat your cereal."

"Oh, that," said Katie. "Sure. Miss Freeman told us about that in school one time."

Then she was satisfied and went on with her breakfast.

"It shows one thing anyway," said Dad.

"What's that?" I asked.

"That wherever he's come from he's been cared for. Those neutering operations cost money."

OK. That's enough about that.

Next his stripeyness. I have to add to what I've said already that the grey behind the black stripes was not any old grey but a yellowish browny grey. This is important, because if we have to advertise him we'd better be precise. There are lots of black-and-grey cats around, but not so many just *this* shade of grey.

Which brings me to his ears.

These are not striped. They are particularly browny—a sandy chocolatey brown that is deeper than anywhere else on him. It seems to me that one of his ancestors might have been a Siamese, because they have ears this colour, some of them.

Another thing about his ears is that they are perfect. Intact, I mean. No cuts or raggediness. Ray was the first to point this out.

"That's very unusual for a full-grown male. It shows that this is a cat who knows how to take care of himself in a fight. Even if it means running away when he knows he'll be licked."

"You old coward, you!" I said to the cat.

"Ngraaow!" agreed the animal, squeezing his eyes proudly.

So next the eyes. Very very clear green, as I have said before. With a habit of squeezing them when you talk kindly to him, as I have mentioned just now. And another habit of opening them wide, when he's not sure about your tone of voice. They have stripes between them in a kind of M pattern, which make him look very anxious when he opens them wide and tenses up like that.

The stripes elsewhere, on his back and his sides, are also nice and even and—what's the word?—like equal, like—

"Symmetrical."

That was Ray's voice butting in.

Yes. Symmetrical.

And on his tail the black comes in rings, the very tip being black. This tip is usually in a slight crook at the end whenever he walks toward you, with the rest of his tail in the air, straight up, which is often.

The stripes also come in thinner, wavier rings around his neck.

But it is the markings around his nose and chin that are the most interesting. His chin is white, but in a thin line all around his mouth it is black. This makes it so that from the side he looks as if he's smiling.

Then, moving on to the end of his nose, this is pink,

without fur, but with one tiny black spot over his left nostril. *That* should really identify him if we have to advertise.

But there is more.

What slays *me*, what really *destroys* me, are some markings in the short grey fur just at the side of his nose. Four more tiny black specks, two on each side of the nostrils. Now I do not mean the black dots that most cats have, him included, where the whiskers sprout, one dot for each whisker. (His are silver and black, mixed.) No. Those are further out on the cheeks.

The ones I am talking about are slap bang over the middle of his mouth, more like dashes than dots, in two pairs, a pair on each side, *and they are just like quote marks ready to go around any speech he makes!*

If only he *could* speak, though. . . .

Then maybe he would tell us exactly where to start making our inquiries tomorrow.

5

SEARCH REPORT

FIRST DAY

FIRST INQUIRY

Before making today's report, I will just recap to bring the record up to date.

SATURDAY — the cat arrived.
SUNDAY — Dad gave his first warning to the girls about feeding the cat.
MONDAY (yesterday) — Dad gave his second warning, this time to us all, and we asked for two days in which to find the cat's true owner.
TUESDAY (today) — has been the first of those two days and this is the report on our search.

First, right after breakfast, we had a meeting to get the details right. We had it out on the porch again. Ray called it a "muster roll." Trina giggled and said it sounded like another name for a hot dog. Ray said he didn't want any more of *that* kind of fooling. He said—well—I recorded the next bit and here it is:

"This is a serious matter."
"Sorry."
"The cat's life might depend on this."
"I said I was sorry, didn't I?"
"OK then. Listen. All of you. Here are your duties. First, I am in command. I direct operations. Right?"
"Right, boss."
"Right, big brother."
"What's operations?"
That was Katie.
Next comes a bit where Trina tries to explain and Ray gets mad and hammers his plaster on the porch rail, but I'll skip that and go to where Ray gets on with the main business.
"Angus, your duty is recording. Not everything, of course. But like when we're asking questions and people are answering. You never know. We may require to check back on the details. OK?"
"OK."
"You sure you have enough tape?"
"Sure."
"The batteries, are they—?"
"Listen. *I'm* the expert on recording. Just leave all that to me, why don't you?"
Well, you have to be firm with Ray about such things or he'll go on and *on*.
"All right. Now Trina. We come to your duty. Very important, this. So will you *please* put that book down?"
"Sorry. My duty. Very important. I was listening. Go on."
"Your duty is to do the first talking. To—"
"How d'you mean?"
"Listen and you'll find out. . . . You are the one who

will introduce us when we go up to inquire of anybody. Being a girl, you see. You will put them at their ease. I will come in later, of course, with my questions. And while you are putting them at their ease I can keep my eyes open and look for signs we might otherwise miss in all the talking. OK?"

(I just have to splice in my comment here and say this. That all this fancy scheme of Ray's about getting Trina to do the talking adds up to one thing. When he first meets strangers, my big brother, Old Boss Man, is chicken. Shy. Not outgoing. Slow to warm up. Call it any of those things Mom and Dad call it, but I still say chicken myself.)

"So what about me? What's my duty?"

Katie.

"You just tag along and keep quiet and—"

"*That's* not a duty!"

"No, it's not, honey!" (This is Trina, who knows much better than Ray how to handle the kid.) "Your duty is Assistant Interviewer, and to notice all the very small but terribly important things that these dum-dum boys are likely to miss!"

Well, that satisfied Katie and we were all set. Here is Ray with his final word:

"The strategy is this. A cat can get lost only a mile away from home, especially if something scares it. I read this in a book once. So at first we search around the farmhouse itself. We go to the nearest neighbours first, before fooling around in any town or village. So we go on foot, the way the cat came. No bikes until or unless we have to search farther afield."

Our nearest neighbour, we knew, lived only about a half mile away. This is Mrs. Urquart, a widow lady. She lives alone up another dirt road leading off the country road. Her house is not a farmhouse, though, but a log cabin, and it is in a clearing in the woods.

We know her name and about her because she is the lady who keeps the spare key to the farmhouse. She also has chickens and we get some of our eggs from her. We all went up in the car last Friday, but stayed in the car while Mom went in, so we only got a glimpse of her then.

She has long grey hair, straight and tumbling over her shoulders like a teen-age girl's, but being grey it looks funny. Her face is all smooth and shiny and scrubbed-looking.

Today she seemed glad to see us and she asked us all into the cabin. It was very hot in there and kind of greeny dark, and it was jammed with old furniture so much that I couldn't begin to tell you what there was, except for a big dark shiny piano. And I only noticed that at first because there was a cat on it—a shaggy all-grey one that looked sleepy and bored and soon put its head down between its paws again.

"Cat, honey? No. This is the only cat I have. Emily. She's thirteen and she's had over one hundred and fifty kittens. How about that?"

"Well, ma'am—"

"Hey now, cut the ma'am, huh? Hetty'll do. Mrs. Urquart even, but not ma'am. All right?"

"Well—uh—Mrs. Urquart—have you *seen* a black-and-grey striped cat around here? Or do you know of one?"

"Black-and-grey striped, huh? Can't say I do, honey. I really can't—Hey, now what's that thing you're pointing at me, son?"

Now "that thing" was the mike, of course. And that did it. That blew one whole hour of our precious searching time.

Because she was all keen to talk into it then, sure, but not about any cat. She was all eager to talk into it about herself, and then to hear it played back.

Here is a sample so you will see the spot we were in.

"I first came here to this cabin here twenty years ago on account of my health. I came from the city, never ask which one, where I had a big house and a car and a maid and everything except the things that mattered. Like my health and—"

Well there's no point in playing more of that, because it had nothing to do with the cat, and it went on, over and over, the same thing. I mean about how she got well in the country and put her roots down here and never once went back to the city, even to sell her house and car and stuff, which she got a lousy price for but she didn't mind because the country air was worth a dollar a sniff. And like that.

It was a bit better when she asked to sing into it. She sang a song about mountains made of rock candy, and another about a Turk and a Russian fighting, with long names. It was better because she gave us some milk and cookies to eat and drink while she sang and played, and besides, to me it was a challenge getting the balance right to record it properly.

But again it has nothing to do with the cat that *I* can figure, so I won't play it in this report.

Instead I will move on to our next inquiry, which was at a motel, our next nearest neighbour, and seemed much more promising.

6

SEARCH REPORT

FIRST DAY

SECOND AND THIRD INQUIRIES

It is not a big motel. It is a small one, privately owned, with only a house and six cabins. It is at the end of the country road and just on the highway. Trina got us all nervy by saying it reminded her of the motel in a movie she once saw when the baby-sitter let us older ones stay up. The movie was called "Psycho" and the man in charge of the motel there murdered some ladies in the shower with a knife.

When Trina mentioned this in the parking lot, Katie screamed and said she was not going in *there*, and she didn't, and she stayed out the whole time, one foot on the highway pavement ready to run for help if he started carving *us* up.

But this man wasn't like the movie man. He was fat and laughing and pleased to see us, and he started right in there kidding as if we'd come to reserve rooms.

"I can offer you our Presidential Suite, or I can let

you have the second-best honeymoon apartment. Which is it to be, young lady?"

"No sir. We have a place already. Just along the road at the Bleeker farm. At least we call it a farm but . . ."

Well, never mind that. It sounds as if Trina was serious, but really she was kidding along too. She does that. Anyone kids her she goes all deadpan and pretends to take it seriously. The motel man soon gave in.

"OK, honey, OK. I was only kidding. What is it I can do for you? Seriously. Can—*say*—!"

He too had noticed the mike and the recorder.

"What is this? An Internal Revenue investigation? You really three forty-year-old agents disguised as kids?"

More fooling around.

Finally we got to tell him about the cat and he became serious again.

No, he and his wife didn't have a cat. A beagle, Freddie, yes.

And no, none of the present guests at the motel had a cat.

One was a travelling salesman for ships' chandlers' merchandise who would never have time to look after any cat while he was on his journeys. And the others were a newly-married couple who'd come straight from their wedding in Boston last Saturday.

"And I guess no one gave them a *striped cat* for a wedding gift! Anyways, they'd have said. And anyways again, if they or the salesman had snuck a cat in for some reason and kept it under wraps, Freddie would have known. That dog *hates* cats and he goes around with my wife every morning to tidy the rooms. He'd have hollered his head off at the least whiff of a cat!"

So that was that.

Our only other near neighbour was a farmer. But don't get me wrong. We had great hopes there. As Ray said, farms carry a whole crew of cats as a rule, inside cats and outside cats. I think he'd been saving it up to the last as our best bet.

But by now it was getting close to lunch time. Here is what Ray said:

"Checking on the farm cats will be a long job. So I say we have lunch first and leave the whole afternoon free if necessary. I have a strong hunch that that is where the cat came from and I want us to be absolutely thorough there."

The farm I am talking about is called the Haywood farm. It is quite a big one. It lies between our farmhouse and the creek. You get to it by going along the road toward the highway, until you come to a dirt road over the fields on the left, the opposite side to us.

One of the reasons Ray had his strong hunch is because the cat first came to us across the field leading down to the road. Of course it could have been circling around for an hour or so, but when we first saw it it was coming from that direction, true enough.

Mr. Haywood is a tall thin man with red hair and bright gold stubbles on his chin. He has two teeth missing in the top, through which he whistles.

He knew us without our saying who we were, and when we told him what we had come about he said this:

"Sure! We have cats. We have eight. Three of them are stripey but I don't know they're so affectionate. They live outdoors save in winter when it's really bad. Anyhow, we'll soon see. . . ."

And then I had to pull the mike away quick, because

he gave such a loud blast of a whistle through the gap in his teeth that he could have destroyed the recorder right then and there.

Two kids came running at the whistle: a boy with red hair, age about ten, and a girl with red hair, age about eight. Both looked very dirty, only with clean farm dirt if you see what I mean, and they wore old blue jeans and T-shirts. He said the boy's name was Nibs and the girl's name was Sherry.

They said "Hi!" but didn't seem very friendly at first. I guess they were really shy. But when their father told them what we wanted they brightened up some and became very interested.

"If he's stripey it could be Jericho, or it could be Terror, or it could be Lucille. Whaddya laughing for?"

Nibs said this to his sister. This is her reply:

"Because if he's a he it sure can't be Lucille."

"No, I guess not."

"Nor is it Terror if his ears are like they say they are. Terror's got half of his right one chewed off."

"So it could be Jericho then."

You can tell from the way Nibs said that that he's the serious type of boy, a bit slow but very thoughtful. Here's what he said next, something that made all of us Bleeker kids' hearts beat faster, I can tell you.

"Come to think, I ain't seen Jericho around much these last few days. You?"

The girl shook her head. The farmer said:

"All right then. So why don't you take our young neighbours here on a tour of the farm? See'f you can see him."

"Wouldn't it be quicker if they came up to our place and saw the cat and—"

That was Trina. If she had not had the sense to break off by herself, I'd have given her a nudge, and I think Ray would have too. Because we were looking forward to that tour of the farm for its own sake, and this was a good excuse.

Anyway, Nibs and Sherry weren't listening. They were running on over to the horse barn (a *much* bigger one than ours) and shouting, "Come on! come on! We'll start right here!"

Well I have to tell you that the tour nearly *ended* right there, also, because one of the first things we saw, nestling in some straw in the barn, was this grey-and-black striped cat called Jericho. And we could tell right away that this wasn't our visitor, who might have found his way back during the morning. No. This one was a silvery grey, and much thinner, and a bit mean looking, and who kept his tail down and hurried away when Katie went to pick him up.

But there was a consolation.

Like the other people we'd talked to, Nibs noticed the recorder. He was a bit slower in coming to it, but when he did, out there in the barn, he was just as interested as Mrs. Urquart had been. Listen:

"You let *me* talk in that thing?"

"Well, we are kind of busy, but—"

"You let me talk in there and—and—I'll let you all have a ride on my pony."

Then his sister chimed in.

"Me too! Please! And you can ride on mine. Mine's quieter 'n his."

Well . . .

Cat or no cat, this was an offer none of us could resist. Not even Boss Man himself.

So we let them record (Nibs did farm animal imitations and Sherry sang "God Bless America") and then we did the tour of the farm after all, all the way down to the creek, over the meadows, past the cows with tinkling bells, and all around, taking it in turns to ride Geronimo, Nibs's pony, a pinto, and Queenie, Sherry's pony, a smaller, brown one.

Honestly, I don't know where the time all went to. Before we knew it, it was five.

Ray told me to switch on the recorder again, back to business.

"Say, Nibs, this has been great. Just great. And many thanks. But we still have to continue our search."

"You're welcome. Do you *have* to go now? Hey! Will you get Geronimo's voice down on that thing? I can make him talk."

He did too. Just touched that pony on the neck someplace and Geronimo gave out this whinney —but everyone knows what a horse sounds like, so I've left it out of my report. Besides, Ray was looking impatient.

"Do you know of any other neighbours around here? Apart from the motel and Mrs Urquart."

Nibs didn't look so sure, but Sherry said:

"There's the trailer lady."

"What trailer lady?"

That was Ray, all keen.

Nibs still wasn't so sure.

"Oh, yeah . . . her. But she don't have a cat. None that I know of anyway."

"Yes, but you never know. Where? Where is she?" (Ray again.)

"Well it's back over to the creek. A little way off of our

land. There's a dirt road runs to it over our fields though. But it's nearly a mile."

We were all feeling tired until Sherry said:

"I know. Why don't we hitch Queenie to the buggy and all ride over there?"

So that's what we did and it was great up there on that buggy and Nibs let us all take turns with the reins. But from the cat point of view—zero.

The trailer was there all right, among some trees on top of a grassy slope just above the creek, near where it joins the river. But the car wasn't with it and the trailer was all shut up.

Nibs said:

"Looks like she's gone someplace else for a few days. But she'll be back. She stays here all summer, every year. On account of her health."

I thought:

"Oh, no! Not another of those!"

I was thinking of the widow lady and all the time and tape she'd taken up with her life story and her songs. I was sort of relieved in a way that this one *wasn't* home. Besides, it didn't sound like she'd be much help over the cat anyway. Listen to this:

"Did she have a cat?"

"None that I heard about. Like I said before. But I wouldn't say she *don't* have one. We just don't get to see her a lot. . . . You've been in there, Sherry, when you've taken her her cream and eggs and stuff. You see any cat?"

"No. No sign at all."

Now she told us!

So that was the end of the first day's search. After supper, Ray said this:

"We wasted too much time this afternoon, I know. But not to worry. We achieved our objective. We covered all the immediate neighbours and that leaves us free tomorrow to go farther afield. Because don't forget. The cat first came up the field, and the field leads to the road, and the road leads to the highway as well as to the farm and the motel. And the highway leads to the town."

"So?"

"So tomorrow we'll concentrate on the town. It's only a one-horse place. Somebody's *sure* to know something there."

7

SEARCH REPORT

SECOND DAY

I sometimes wish we had our stereo here with us. Then I could play background music to these reports.

For *this* one, I tell you, I would pick a Funeral March, I think.

Because, well, for starters, our investigations in the town were tougher than we'd thought.

Small the place may be, compared to Philadelphia. One-*horse*, as Ray said, maybe. But being a river town and this being the middle of summer, it sure wasn't a one-*car* town. There were zillions of them, mainly tourist cars, and with the streets being so narrow—just wide enough to fit that one horse, some of them—it made biking along them very tricky at times.

Then don't forget this. About a half of those zillion cars stopped by in town, and people got out of them and strolled around, looking at antiques shops or for places to eat and drink, or simply just to take pictures down by the quay. And that brings me to my second point.

Down by that quay there were about a million boats, and they don't drive or sail themselves, either. They all need people to run them, and most of these people were out on the streets, too, taking pictures or looking for antiques, etc.

So it was very difficult knowing who to question. I mean the cat's come from a home, right? So we needed to talk with people who had homes in that area, right?

But just how do you sort them out from the tourists and transients?

Listen. Out of the first ten people we stopped and asked, *nine* of them were from faraway places and the tenth was a nut.

We'd worked it out. "Begin by asking if they live in town," Ray told Trina. "Then we won't waste time," he said. So we did. And here are those first ten answers:

1. "We're from New York, but thanks for the compliment."
2. "Sorry, no. Toronto. We're just passing through."
3. "I—air—how to say—hee! hee!—we not even live in zees *country*, ma'mselle!"
4. "Good heavens, no! What gave you that idea?"
5. "I only wish we *did*! This is a *beautiful* town, little girl, and I hope you all appreciate living here."
6. "No, but we're hoping to live here when we retire."
7. "We *look* like hicks or somethin'?"
8. "Whu? Nuh-huh! And could you *please* direct me to a dentist?"
9. "First time in my life I set foot in the place."

And then came the nut. A tall man with a mournful yellow face.

"Yeah. I live here."

"Good. I wonder if you could help us, sir?"

"If it's money, no. You got a nerve to ask. Do I look like I was made of money? No, I—"

"It isn't money, sir, no. It's about a cat, a—"

"*Cat?* You talk to *me* about a *cat*? New-fangled, weekend, amateur, Sunday-sailor, clumsy-lookin', no-good contraptions! I *hate* 'em!"

And he walked away, still muttering.

It was Ray who realized in the end that the sort of "cats" he meant, and thought *we* meant, was the boats they call "cats," short for "catamarans."

"I guess he's the old-fashioned type of sailing man."

Maybe. But I still think he was some kind of a nut. I mean it was just as if he'd never heard of regular cats, with four legs, and whiskers, and fur, and big green eyes.

After that we stopped fooling around with passers-by. The morning was wearing on by then. So we spent the rest of the time questioning people we knew for a fact were citizens and home-owners of that town. The people in the stores and places, behind the counters.

Well, at least we weren't wasting time any more, but I can't say we got much further. Nearly all of them were patient with us and listened to our descriptions. Two of them even called up neighbours they knew had a cat like this one, which they couldn't remember seeing around lately. And they nearly all promised to make further inquiries and let us know if they heard of a black and grey stripey that had gone missing since Friday or Saturday or thereabouts.

But definite news there was none. Both places where the store clerks phoned through said no, their cats were safe home: one lying in the sun in the front-room windowsill; and the other making a nuisance of itself right now because it didn't care for the cat food they'd put down that morning.

We kept plugging away after lunch, back in town, right into the middle of the afternoon. But still no definite news. Here's what we said then, sitting drinking cokes on the quayside on a bench outside the tavern when we finally took a break. Trina first:

"Well, we tried!"

Then Ray:

"Sure. And much good it's done us."

Trina:

"Oh, I don't know. We've got a lot of the townspeople looking out for us now. All those who promised to ask around."

"Sure. Great. But you're forgetting one thing."

"What's that?"

"That we only have until tonight. Today's Wednesday, remember. What's the use if one of these people does find out where the cat came from, say on Friday, if he's been collected by the ASPCA already?"

"Well—huh—well probably the ASPCA don't put them to sleep immediately. Probably there'll still be time for the owners to go around to the pound and collect him, even if it isn't until Friday we get to hear."

"Hmm! I wouldn't like to bet on it."

"Me neither!" This was Katie. In the background, that was her coke can she let drop to the floor in her anxiety. "What are we all waiting for?"

So we kept plugging away, plugging away.

We even had the bright idea of going to the Post Office, knowing the mailmen would visit practically every home in the area during the course of a few days.

Well, no one had heard anything there, either. But they were very sympathetic. The man at the counter made a note of all we told him. He said:

"Now if it was a dog that had gone missing, the men might not be so willing to help, the problems some dogs give them. But a cat, sure. I'll ask them to keep their ears open, ask around. Then I'll let you know. The old Percival place you're at, isn't it, over by the Haywood farm?"

And that was the last stop we made this afternoon, because it was getting late. Even Katie was ready to call it a day and hope that by the time we got home one of our earlier inquiries would have proved successful. Trina gave her the idea.

"You never know, honey," she said. "One of those people in the stores might have seen someone in the meantime who *has* lost a cat like ours. And they might already have driven around to the farm to collect it. They might even be there now, at this moment."

Well at least it gave poor Katie a bit more energy to pedal her bike with on the journey home.

And on that journey home we made an unexpected inquiry.

Just inside the country road where it turns off the highway was a trooper's car. The trooper was sitting in it watching the traffic go by.

"Hey, why don't we ask *him*?" said Ray. "He'll get around all over the area. He might have heard something . . . . Trina . . . ."

But Trina was already doing her thing.

I didn't record this inquiry. The trooper was a young man with very piercing blue eyes, and although he smiled when Trina stuck her head in at the window I thought maybe he might not like having a microphone stuck in his face as well.

Anyway, he hadn't much to say. And what he did say wasn't much help. In fact it was the opposite. In fact it was so much the opposite, such Bad News, that it stuck in our minds as clearly as any recording. He said:

"I'm sorry, and I'd sure like to help, and of course if I do hear of someone looking for a cat of that description I'll let you know. But from what you tell me, it looks like he could have been dumped."

"Dumped?"

We stared at him.

This was something new.

"Sure," he said. "It happens all the time. People get tired of an animal and instead of doing the proper thing and taking it to a veterinarian or the ASPCA to be painlessly killed, they dump it. Usually out on a country road like this. Usually at night so no one sees them. And far enough from home so the animal can't find its way back."

I tell you.

The Funeral March.

That's what I should be playing in back of this.

And of course it didn't cheer us up any when we got back and found the cat still there, sitting on the porch, with nobody having been to claim him as Trina had hoped, but squeezing his eyes at us as if he was glad to see us and everything was great, just great, and Ray said:

"There's another thing that isn't so good, either."

"Oh, no! There's *more*?"

"If he *was* dumped . . ."

"Well?"

"Well can't you see what that means? It means that even if we did find the owners, they wouldn't want him back. He'd still be thrown out again—or—well—put to sleep."

Katie started to cry. She had scooped up the cat and he was speedboating in her arms and suddenly her tears began to splash into his fur.

Trina put one arm around her and stroked the cat with her other hand.

"Don't cry, honey. It may not have been like that at all. . . ." Then to Ray and me, she said: "We'll still go on trying, anyway. We just can't let Daddy call the ASPCA *now*. We have to plead for an extension whether we like it or not."

"Oh gosh, there's *that*!" said Ray, tapping his plaster cast on the porch rail. "I'd forgotten."

So had I.

But Trina was right.

So the next report you get from me will be tonight, after we've made that plea, and I sure hope I don't feel like playing a Funeral March with *that*.

Though better not count on it.

Dad can be pur-retty stubborn when it comes to anyone going back on a deal they've made with him.

8

THE NEW DEAL

We made our pitch before supper.

This was Mom's idea. I guess we would have put it off as long as possible, but she said:

"As soon as you've washed up we'll talk about it. The whole family. I am not having a meal spoiled by haggling and hassling at the table."

Dad agreed. He was looking very grim. Quiet but grim.

"Sooner we get it over, the better."

So we washed up, which at this place means taking a big pitcher of hot water to our rooms, with big china bowls with flower patterns on them. We usually find this fun, but not this evening, of course. Not with this big meeting hanging over us, on which the cat's life depended.

We held the meeting in the front room, which Mom likes to call the "parlour" on account of its being in an old farmhouse, but which had a new angle tonight because it sounds like "parley" and a parley is when two enemy sides get together to talk terms.

Dad presided. Who else? He presided sitting in the rocking chair, which I guess is as near he can get to his judge's chair back home. He had that same look on his face, too, very severe and determined, with his hands palm down on the table in front of him.

Mom sat on a fine old genuine antique milking stool, in a corner by the bureau desk.

We kids just sat or stood around. You know . . .

One more member present, or nearly present, was the cat. He sat on the windowsill outside, blinking through the screen at us and making faint bubbling noises whenever Katie or Trina or Mom spoke. I know this because I was standing near there, leaning against the wall, with my recorder at the ready on the bookcase ledge.

I did not have the mike ready as well, though, for reasons which I will be coming to soon.

Anyway, Ray led off as planned, coming straight out with it, saying something like this:

"Honestly, sir, we've been working like dogs, all of the two days, and all we need right now is a little extra time. We feel sure we're close to a breakthrough."

Dad didn't move. Still hunched. Still grim.

"You asked for two days and I gave you two. That was the deal. You all agreed."

"Yes, sir. But this is tougher than we thought. All we're asking for is a little more time."

"A deal is a deal."

"Sure, yes! But like if someone owes someone some-

thing and the date due comes around and he just doesn't have it, not all of it. Why then, it's normal to give him a bit longer to pay. It's only the Mafia in the movies that don't give extra time."

"My son the bilker!" said Dad, scowling.

"What's a bilker?" said Katie.

"One who wants out when dues-day comes. One who goes back on his word."

"My father the loan-shark!" muttered Ray.

"*What was that*?" growled Dad, looking up sharp.

"Nothing, sir. Sorry. Just thinking aloud."

Then Trina weighed in. I guess she could see Ray was getting nowhere. Her eyes went as big as an owl's and her bottom lip trembled and she said:

"If that cat is put to sleep just because nobody would give us a few extra days, then as soon as I'm old enough I shall go into a convent—or—or a hermitage. And I shall take a vow of silence and I shall never see any of you again!"

(This I recognized. It was like what the heroine did in a historical story Trina had been reading. Only in the book it had been in *aid* of her father, not against him, when an evil baron had come and taken all the father's land.)

Anyway, it didn't have much effect on *our* father. He just grunted. Even smiled a bit, I think.

"I *shall*, you know!" said Trina, looking mad, as two tears began to flow.

Then Katie weighed in.

"Yes, and *I'll* run away! I'll run away with the cat and hide in the woods before they come to kill him. And we'll live together in a little hut and I'll never speak to you again!"

Katie—who daren't go to the outhouse in the dark!

Dad didn't cave in at that threat, either.

So all right—what did *I* say?

I bet that's what you're thinking.

Well, I said nothing and I do not mind admitting it.

My contribution was going to speak for itself.

You see, I knew that if Ray or Trina or Katie (his favourite) didn't succeed, I wouldn't stand much of a chance. No. I knew that if *they* all failed, our only hope was to get Mom on our side.

So far she had said nothing. But now I was going to jog her memory, prick her conscience. Remember me getting her to say on the recorder how she had been partly to blame, feeding the cat, etc.? Well now I was going to play it back.

I had found the place on the tape and I was going to trigger it off, very dramatically, and see what effect that would have. And *that* is why I wasn't recording this session—why I have to remember what everybody said. I mean you just can't have the recorder ready to play back *and* record at the same time.

OK.

So there it was, all ready to go, with my finger on the release, when Mom spoke up live and beat me to it. And what she said I shall always remember, because it makes me feel like a jerk for ever thinking it was necessary to play a trick on her to get her on our side.

"Clyde," she said, "I think we ought to look at this logically."

"That's what I am doing. The emotion is all coming from *them* . . . . Convents! Hiding in the woods! Mafia!"

"Yes, well. They have a point. Ray is quite right. They *have* put a lot of work in. They *have* tried. And don't you think it would be terrible if some of that work starts bearing fruit? I mean if, as a result of their inquiries, someone comes along in a day or two and claims the cat. Only to find the cat has already been destroyed."

Ray slapped his right hand against the plaster on his left.

"Right on! I was going to say just that, before Dad put me off with his—"

Mom waved him quiet, still looking hard at Dad.

"Don't you agree, Clyde?"

He sighed. He shoved the tips of his fingers up between his eyes and his glasses and rubbed gently.

"Yes, but there's the moral issue," he said. "Kids should know that when they make a deal it's a *deal*!"

"Clyde! There are deals and deals. It isn't some odd job they promised to do by tonight. It isn't even the repayment of a loan. They're acting out of kindness. It's a harmless living creature's *life*."

He had another rub at this.

"Oh, well . . ." He shook his head. "I don't know . . ."

She'd got him! She'd got him!

But we know our father. We knew not to show our triumph too soon. And that was a good thing. Because he still had another argument. A powerful argument. The trooper's argument.

Speaking a lot kindlier, he said:

"Look, kids, I overheard what some of you were saying when you were coming in. About speaking to that trooper. Well, he's right, you know. The chances are that the cat was dumped deliberately. And if that is so, why, even if you trace the owners it won't save the cat."

But again Mom came to the rescue.

"I've been giving that some thought, too," she said.

"And you know what I think? I think the chances are *against* that theory. I mean look at him. He's been too well cared for. He's a mature well-cared-for cat, not an unwanted kitten. And you said yourself that he's had money spent on him."

"Oh, well . . ."

"So I suggest that we let the kids have more time. Give them the rest of the vacation, if necessary. That's ten whole days, and—"

"Let's hear it for Mom, you guys!"

"Yeah!"

"Hurray for Mom!"

"Hurray—"

"Wait!" Mom was looking flushed but serious. "Just one thing. Remember, all of you, that we can *not* take him back with us. If you don't find his home by then, I shall be just as firm as your father."

"We'll find it, we'll find it!"

"Sure we'll—"

"Wait!" she said again. Then turned to Dad. "Is that agreed, Clyde?"

He was nodding already.

"OK, OK. I guess it is only logical."

"And don't forget this too, honey: it is giving them all something to do together. You said yourself you like to see them working as a team."

Ray caught on.

"Yes," he said. "And there's this too, Dad—it's sure helping us to get to know the locality."

Trina joined in.

"Yes, and it's helping us to get acquainted with the neighbours. And make new friends like Nibs and Sherry and—"

"All *right* already!" Dad slammed the table. "I agreed, didn't I? Satisfied?"

Ray gave us the nod and we all went up to Dad and thanked him. Trina and Katie kissed him.

But it was Mom who deserved all that really, and we thanked her after supper by helping her with the dishes without being asked. I also said it out loud—still feeling a bit of a jerk for not trusting her right from the start—and she laughed and said:

"Oh well, I guess I just couldn't bear the thought of Trina becoming a hermit. How could she ever achieve her life's ambition *then*?"

Trina blinked.

"Which ambition is that, Mom? I mean besides finding a home for the cat?"

"Why, you know!" said Mom. "The one you told me about last week. About becoming the United States first woman President. That's no job for hermits. . . . Then again, I couldn't bear the thought of Katie and the cat getting lost together in those spooky woods. I mean it's a lot easier looking for one big thing like a home than for two small things like a cat and a little girl."

Well that sounded logical too.

But, as Ray whispered to me, sounding worried again:

"It *is* a lot easier. If you know where to start *looking* for that home!"

He's right.

Ten more days sounds like all the time in the world to a kid like Katie and a dreamer like Trina.

But we guys know it'll soon slip by and that we can't afford to ease up now for one hour.

Not if that cat is to go on living after we return to Philadelphia!

9

THE CAT COMES IN

That meeting took place on Wednesday evening. Right now, when I am making this report, it is Friday evening.

"So what has happened in the meantime?"

I can hear people asking that question. Also these:

"Why the gap?"—and:

"Why no report for all of forty-eight hours?"

I can also hear them wondering. I can hear them wondering about two things especially.

One:

"Has he been too busy since Wednesday night to make a report? And as a result of being so busy, is it all over? Have they *found* the cat's owner?"

Two:

"Or has he forgotten what he said on Wednesday night and started taking it easy, thinking ten days is plenty of time?"

Well, I will tell you the correct answer.

The correct answer is: Yes. We have been very busy. Very busy indeed.

The first thing that made us so busy was on Wednesday night itself, when the cat was allowed in officially.

I say "officially" because up until then it had been strictly forbidden to enter the house. Both Mom and Dad had been firm about this.

"All right," Mom had said. "You may feed it. You may see that it doesn't starve. But you must do nothing to make it feel at home. That would raise its hopes too high. That *would* be cruel."

So between Saturday morning and Wednesday evening, the cat took all its meals outside. It took them on the front porch, which it seemed to like the best of all places. Between meals, that is where it used to be mostly, lying on the bare boards, gazing out on the sea of grass in the field, watching the wind brush over it and make waves. There it would lie, gazing out over the field, as if expecting to see his owners show up, his green eyes gleaming between the white rails, except if we ourselves happened to be coming up the dirt road.

Then he would slowly get up, arch his back, and yawn.

And when we got close enough, he would stretch and come and meet us with his tail in the air.

"Just like he was our own!" Trina used to say.

"And so he is!" Katie would croon, as she put out her arms and the cat came to her.

It was always to Katie he would come first, right from the start.

"That kid's going to break her heart over this!" I heard Dad say once.

"Well there's nothing much we can do about it right now," was Mom's reply.

When we went into the house ourselves the cat would often try to follow us. Sometimes it did get in, but not for long. Dad was *very* strict about this. Mom was nearly as bad. Especially when Katie was the last to enter did they keep sharp watch, because those were the times that the screen doors were mostly left ajar.

"If I'd known about this I'd have had springs fitted on those doors," Dad said, on the fifth or sixth time he had to put the cat out.

So when the cat wasn't lying on the porch, his white chin flat on the boards and his green eyes staring through the white rails, he seemed mostly to be on the windowsill of whatever room most of us were in at the time. It was a bit uncanny in a way—almost as if we were all prisoners and he was the guard, making sure we didn't run away ourselves. And maybe it *was* something like that, too. Maybe right from the start that cat was pinning all his hopes on us, and wanting to make sure *we* didn't desert him, whoever else had.

All this was during the day and in the evenings.

Nights, the cat was supposed to be sleeping under the porch.

"It's dry there, even after the storm," Mom said on Saturday afternoon. "I don't see why he shouldn't be comfortable."

"But there might be *bears*!" said Katie.

"Nonsense!" said Mom.

"Bears don't eat cats!" said Trina, who ought to know, the number of animal books she's read.

So Katie gave in on condition that she was allowed to fix a bed for the cat under the porch, in a carton filled with old sweaters, which she found in a chest in the girls' bedroom, and which Mom wasn't sure about on account she thought they might have been left there by our cousins Meriol and Judy, ready for Thanksgiving.

But Katie had her way and the "bed" was made up and shoved under the cat's nose out on the porch, so he could sniff it and realize it was his. He didn't seem all *that* interested, I must say. Just a couple of sniffs and then he yawned and turned his back on it and had a wash. But we put it in a dry part under the porch just the same and—sure enough—the next morning, Sunday, the sweaters were all crushed down and seemed to have been slept on.

Ha!

I said "seemed." And earlier I said "the cat was *supposed*" to be sleeping under the porch. And earlier yet I said Wednesday night was the first time the cat was allowed in "*officially.*"

Because you know what?

It was all baloney.

It was all baloney because on Wednesday night, when the cat was *invited* in, you know where he headed first? Straight for the girls' room is where.

And you know *where* in the girls' room he headed first?

Katie's bunk.

Mom is always telling us to make our beds every morning. Well, some of us do and some of us don't bother. Katie is one of those who don't unless they have to. Being the youngest she has an excuse, I guess, but on Wednesday night I bet she wished she had been more regular about it.

Because her bed wasn't made. And there, at the foot

of it, in the patchwork quilt, was a perfect hollow, exactly the size of the cat when he's curled up.

Ray picked him up, just before he was about to leap up and into that hollow.

"Just a minute!" he said. "It looks like he's been here before."

"Shut the door!" whispered Trina.

"Why, there are cat hairs in this hollow," said Ray. "And bits of dried mud like from between a cat's toenails!"

"Oh, please, Ray, not so loud!" said Katie.

"All right then," said Ray—who can get almost as bossy as Dad at times. "Come clean. How long?"

"Since Saturday night," confessed Trina.

"He tapped at the window ever so gently," said Katie.

"He was so polite," said Trina. "We just couldn't refuse to open the screen."

"And then he came in," said Katie.

"Straight for the bottom bunk as if he'd slept there all his life," said Trina.

So the bed under the porch was all phooey. Katie and Trina had faked that hollow in the sweaters themselves, to make it look as if he was sleeping there.

"All right," said Ray. "So from now on you keep no secrets from the rest of us. This is a team operation, OK?"

They agreed.

"So long as you don't tell Daddy."

We ignored that. It went without saying.

"By the way," I said. "Weren't you taking a big risk? I mean if he'd wanted to go to the bathroom?"

"They'd leave the screen open," said Ray. "Didn't you?"

The girls shook their heads and looked at each other.

"Nuh-huh!" said Trina. "I wanted to, but Katie has this thing about vampires. She insisted on closing it."

"So?" I said, looking at the cat, now curled up in the hollow on Katie's bed and licking his paws carefully. "Like I said. You were taking a risk."

Again Trina shook her head. This time Katie giggled.

"Look!" she said.

And from under the bunk she drew out a flat wood box, the sort they use for seeds, which boxes there's a stack of in the horse barn. It was filled with dry dirt.

"Kitty's bathroom," she said.

"He uses it ever so neatly!" said Trina. "That was something else he took to straight off."

Ray looked very thoughtful, but said nothing.

It was only later he told us what was on his mind.

Thursday—yesterday—we spent pretty much like Wednesday. That is to say we made a town search. This time, though, it was a different town.

Where we are is between two townships. The one we visited on Wednesday is only about three miles away. That is why we went there first, because it is nearer.

Today, however, we decided to try the other, which is about six miles away in the other direction, once you get to the highway.

Because it is so far away we might not have bothered, if we hadn't been given this ten days' extension. But as Ray said:

"Now that we do have extra time, it is our duty to be all the more thorough."

"*Six or seven miles*, though!" said Trina, who'd just started another book.

"Cats do stray that far," said Ray. "If something scares them enough."

"Can't I stay home and play with him and make sure nothing else scares him?" said Katie.

"No!" said Ray. "This is a team operation."

"And you might be the one who asks the very question that finds out who his true owners are, honey," said Trina.

Which satisfied Katie immediately.

So we went to this other town and we took a picnic lunch and we stayed there the whole day. And the reason I haven't used up a lot of tape to make a report on *that* day's search is because it was so much like the other.

Another river town.

Another zillion cars.

Another million boats.

And most of the people in the streets only visitors.

This time, though, we didn't waste time on *them*. We headed straight for the stores, the lunch counters, the Post Office, and so on.

Again, no one actually *knew* of a missing cat, but again a lot of them promised to inquire for us.

So we weren't downhearted at the end of the day.

Ray said it.

"Now we have *really* covered the area. Now there are all sorts of people in all directions looking out for us."

Trina seemed relieved.

"Good. So now we can just sit back and relax and wait for someone to come and claim him. Or at least to give us information that will tell us where to inquire next."

Ray looked mad.

"We can *not* then! . . . Honestly!" He groaned and rolled his eyes at me. "Look. Listen. All of you. We can lay off the leg work, yes. We needn't go on any more search inquiries for a day or two, sure. But by golly we'll not waste time. We'll *use* it."

We all looked a bit puzled.

"How?" I asked.

And that's when Ray told us what had occurred to him, what had made him so thoughtful, hearing about the cat and its bed and its bathroom on Wednesday night.

"We can use the next few days to make a thorough study of the cat itself. His habits. What he seems used to. What turns him on. What scares him. What just doesn't interest him. To study him like that might give us all sorts of clues about where he came from and all his past life. Then we could really narrow our search down. *Really* pinpoint it."

10

AMNESIA?

Well, that was last night, Thursday night. And I want to tell you that Ray couldn't have picked a better time for announcing his plan. Because today has sure been a good day for a "really thorough systematic investigation of the cat itself."

Why?

Because it has rained all day is why. And I do mean rained and I do mean all day.

No storm. No thunder and lightning. No torrents. No roaring winds.

But good, steady rain.

"Well I'm glad to see you all looking so cheerful about it," Mom said, right after breakfast, when normally we'd have been staring out of the window and looking up at the sky and sighing hard and crossing our fingers.

"Cheerful" maybe wasn't the right word. But "alert,"

"eager," "on the ball"—any of those would have been fine.

Because that's what we were. All set. Me with my recorder and Trina with a notebook and Katie on her knees, hovering over the cat. All we needed was for him to start moving around, doing things, showing us the habits he's got, and other peculiarities. Anything which might help to give a clue about his true home.

But you know what?

At first it looked as if he would *never* get started. He just lay there, over by the stove, stretched out on the bare boards which—except at nights—he seems to prefer to chairs and cushions.

"Should we stir him up?" said Trina.

Ray said "No!" so loud that it very nearly *did* stir the cat up. He lifted his head and pricked his ears and stared. Then blinked and yawned and got his head down again.

"No," said Ray, in a quieter voice. "It has to be natural. What he does *naturally*. You can't force things."

"I guess you could say *that* was a special thing about him," I said.

"What?"

"Preferring to lie on bare boards during the day."

"Yeah," said Ray. "Good thinking, Angus. Make a note of it."

After that, while we waited for the cat to get up and move around naturally, we spent the time trying to put together all we had gotten so far about his habits and likings. To do this, we all thought very hard, and racked our brains, and tried to remember this and that. But one of the best ways, we soon decided, was to play back the whole of the record this far, and so we did, and we were right, because it helped us remember all kinds of things.

Here is what we came up with, after that playback.

First, of course, all the things I'd mentioned in my report on "The Cat's Description." Like being male, striped black and grey, green eyes, large build, fully grown, neutered, affectionate with girls and women, cautious without being too timid.

"So I think that two things we can definitely count on," said Ray, "are that the home he came from is a good one, and that it included at least one woman and/or girl. OK?"

We all agreed.

Ray nodded, looking very pleased with himself.

"I think we can also say that it is not an old woman, living alone."

We weren't so sure about that one.

"Why?"

Ray scratched at the rim of his plaster thoughtfully.

"Well at one time I thought it had to be. After what the trooper said, and what Mom said about what the trooper said."

"Oh?"

"Yeah. I didn't want to worry you guys or anything. But I could see a way that he could have come from a good home *and* been dumped."

Mom had just come into the room. She looked as interested as any of us.

"Go on," she said.

"Well," said Ray, "all right. He's come from a good home where he was well looked after. OK. And he's been given lots of affection, right? So Mom was right.

Owners like that wouldn't dump him. They wouldn't even *give* him away, I bet."

"So?"

Ray looked around, very serious but also very pleased with himself still. He paused, so that all we could hear was the rain drumming down and the rattle of Dad's newspaper in the parlour.

"But supposing someone *died*," said Ray. "Huh? Supposing his loving owner *died*?"

Trina gasped.

"*Murdered?*" she whispered.

Ray shook his head, smiling his pitying smile.

"No. Just died. An old lady who dies. So what happens? Her relatives come along to see to her belongings, sort out her furniture, share it. But they don't like cats, don't want him. Or maybe they're like us—not allowed to keep animals where they live. Yet they don't feel like having him put to sleep. Maybe too poor or too miserly to pay for it. Maybe too ashamed, knowing the old lady would have wanted him to live on. So they dump him. They bring him out into the country and—'Goodbye, cat! You're on your own, old buddy!'."

"Gosh! Yes!" said Trina.

"*So why didn't you tell us this Wednesday night?*" came Dad's voice, from the parlour.

Ray was shaking his head, though.

"Because, likely as it sounds, that wasn't the way it happened. I went on figuring it out and I realized that an old lady's cat almost certainly wouldn't be used to children. And anyway, if there were children visiting so often that it did get used to them—grandchildren, neighbours—why, *they* would take him over when she died. One of them at least. No problem. . . . So it wasn't an old lady who died."

"My brother the detective!" said Trina.

"Look, he's getting up!" said Katie just then, meaning the cat.

During the next hour or so, we watched that cat eat, lap up milk, wash, scratch himself, and watch us back.

Nothing much really, except that every moment we expected to be able to make some other tremendous deduction, so we still remained keen and alert.

Then:

"Hey, where's he going *now*?"

The atmosphere was like that. Even an ordinary thing like moving into another room had us all excited.

He was going into the girls' bedroom, which is on the first floor, leading off the kitchen and opposite the parlour. Straight through the open door he went and to the bottom bunk, then he turned his head.

"Yeeip!" he went, looking straight at Katie.

Katie lifted him up.

"Maybe he wants to go to bed," she murmured. "Does he then?" she said, nuzzling the cat and putting him in his quilt hollow.

But no.

He jumped straight out of it and back on the floor and stood there and gave his faint sharp mew again.

"I bet I know," said Trina. "He wants his bathroom tray."

And she bent down and pulled it from under the bunk.

Sure enough, he went straight onto it and sat and made a small slow puddle.

"Hey!" said Mom through the doorway. "That's only for nights."

But the cat had finished by then, and very neatly too. Then he covered it all up without spilling a single crumb of dirt over the edge.

"Now *that*," said Ray, looking all excited, "is *tremendously* interesting."

"I'm glad you think so," Mom said a bit sarcastically.

"No. Seriously," said Ray. "Don't you see what it means? Most cats ask to go out to do that, right? They go to the outside door and ask to be let out. Grown cats do, anyway."

"So?"

"So don't you *see*? This cat is used to using a tray at all times—day or night."

"But—" began Katie, looking puzzled.

"You mean—?" began Trina, suddenly looking *not* puzzled.

"I mean like a cat in a city apartment. Where they *never* go out."

Again we all stared at him. Even over in the parlour everything was very quiet now.

"My brother the *great detective!*" said Trina, staring up at him with shining eyes.

Well all right. I too thought it was a smart bit of thinking. But it was beginning to look like a complicated picture we were building up if the cat did come from a big city apartment. Why, the nearest place of that sort must be—what?—fifteen, twenty miles away!

After that, it looked like another long wait for revelations, because the cat went back into the kitchen, had another wash, then lay down on the boards and went to sleep again.

But no.

After about ten minutes there was an interruption. Visitors.

"Who—?" began Mom, when she opened the kitchen outer door and saw them standing dripping in the summer kitchen.

"I'm Nibs and this is Sherry, ma'am. And this here's Charlie. We been told not to come in, just to give you these, a gift from Mom, she's waiting down in the car, and how's Ray and Angus and the other two and did they find out about the cat yet?"

The "these" they'd brought us turned out to be a box of fresh-laid eggs (twenty-four, all brown ones). And the "Charlie" was—no, not another Haywood kid—a kind of sheep dog.

"Oh, dear!" cried Mom, as he stepped past her, jingling his medal, into the kitchen. "The cat!"

"He's used to cats, ma'am," said Nibs. "*C'm here, ya jerk!*"

He said that last a lot calmer than the words themselves would make you think. And calmly Charlie turned and went back behind Nibs.

"Yes," said Ray, next to me. "And the cat is used to dogs. Look!"

It had waked up and it had sat up. But that was all. It was sitting up still, in the same place, just looking watchful at the door, but not a bit panicky. You could tell from the dog's wet paw marks how close he'd come to the cat, even if you'd not been watching. About three feet is all.

So that was something else we'd learned.

"We can't be absolutely sure, of course," said Ray. "But the chances are that in the home it comes from there is also a dog."

"Or being an apartment cat all his life," said Trina, "he's just never come into contact with dogs and hasn't learned to treat them as enemies."

The next major discovery was made by Katie. Or at least it was because of her that the next major discovery was made.

It was after lunch.

He had jumped onto her lap where she was sitting, in the parlour rocking chair, and she was singing to him softly and stroking him, and he was sitting like the Sphinx, longwise, facing outward, paws tucked under his chest and squeezing his eyes open and shut like crazy.

"Pure bliss!" said Mom.

"Yeah—well—"

Ray wasn't all that impressed. He glanced at his watch, impatient for the cat to start moving around, ready for more revelations.

Then Katie said:

"I wonder what *caused* this though?"

She was rubbing between the cat's ears with the tip of a finger.

"Caused what?"

"This crack thing."

Katie made her finger rub slowly lengthways, tracing a path along the middle of the cat's head down to his neck.

"You mean the markings?" I said. "Who knows what causes cats' markings?"

Dumb kid! I thought.

"No. She means the crack in his skull," said Trina.

We stared at her.

This was the first that any of the rest of us had heard of it. I guess it was because the girls were always petting him and stroking him that they'd found it.

"Here, let me feel!" said Ray.

"Be careful then."

Ray was careful.

"Gosh, they're right!" he said. "Here, Angus. You feel."

I felt the cat's head. Sure enough, under the fur, instead of the skull being smooth there was a kind of thin ridge, like the seam on a baseball.

"That cat has had a nasty crack at one time or another," said Ray.

"Maybe even a fractured skull," I said.

"Poor thing!" crooned Katie.

"I'd say *definitely* a fractured skull," said Trina.

"Oh, sure, sure!" growled Ray. "*Now* you say it. But why didn't you mention it before?"

"I didn't think," said Trina. "It was late one night when we first noticed it, then in the morning I forgot. What's the big deal, anyway? It's obviously a very old injury. He doesn't mind you touching it at all."

"Yes," said Ray. "But an old *head* injury—that could be tremendously important."

"How?"

"Why, brain damage, of course!"

Katie looked up—very fierce.

"This cat is *not* a nut!"

"I didn't say it was. But an injury like that could have left it with loss of memory. Not all the time, but every now and then. Maybe that's why he strayed. It happens to humans. They call it amnesia."

"Yurrup!"

Ray stared. We all stared.

The cat had stopped squeezing his eyes and was now looking very alert, straight at Ray.

"He's agreeing with you," said Katie. "You must be right."

"In a pig's eye he is!" said Ray, very excited. "It was the word that did it. . . . *Amnesia*. . . . See?!"

The cat hadn't spoken this time, but its ears had pricked up.

"That's not a cat name!" said Trina, looking as if she wished she'd made the discovery.

"No, but I bet it's something pretty close," said Ray.

So then started the naming of the names. We stood around and bombarded that cat with names to see if it would react. It was a bit like detectives giving a suspect the third-degree, only gentler of course. A *gentle* bombardment.

First we tried names that sounded just like "Amnesia."

"Caesar!"

"Breezer!"

"Beezer!"

"Teaser!"

Even girls' names after a while, in case he'd been given it before they realized he was male.

"Teresa!"

"Tricia!"

"Delesia!"

Flower names, too.

"Fresia!"

"Aubretia!"

And plain fool names.

"Squeeze–ya!"

"Sneezier!"

And like that—none of which had an effect, I have to admit.

Even Dad wasn't much more successful.

"Shalmaneser!" he said, sticking his head in at the door.

The cat's ears pricked up slightly, but his eyes were closed and his chin was dipped well down.

"What kind of a name is that?" said Katie.

"A king's name," Dad said. "King of Assyria."

"The chances are that its name does have *ss* sounds in it," Mom said. "They're very popular with cats. It's the *ss* sound that catches their attention."

"Maybe that's all it was with Amnesia," I said.

"I'm not so sure," said Ray. "But anyway, it's a good enough temporary name. Till we find the right one for sure, which will only be when we trace his owner. So I say that from now on we call him Amnesia. All right?"

For once, every single member of the family agreed on something without hesitation. It sounded so right. It sounded so right that if Amnesia *isn't* the cat's real name, then it goshdarn well ought to be!

Anyway, that's what it is with us now, and always will be, no matter what.

And I guess that's it for today's report. I mean that is all by way of truly *positive* discoveries.

The cat went to sleep. The rain continued coming down. And we all still went on trying.

"I wonder if there's anything more we've missed," said Ray. "Anything we might have noticed but forgot to mention. Like certain dum-dums did about the crack."

So we sat quiet and closed our eyes and tried to remember.

"Well," said Trina slowly, after a while.

"Well what?" said Ray. "Don't tell me you've been keeping something *else* back?"

She shook her head.

"No. Nothing definite. Just sort of—well—maybe I just imagined it. But when he first came, that first morning, and I first picked him up, I seemed to catch a trace of perfume."

"Perfume? Anyone else? Katie?"

"No. But Trina's very good at smells."

"Oh, I don't know," said Trina. "He did have pollen on him, if you remember. It could have been that."

"Even so, it could bear out our theory that his owner was a woman, and you should have mentioned it before," said Ray. "Anything else?"

"Well," I said, "it's too late now. But I wish we'd thought at the time to examine Amnesia's feet."

"What for?" asked Katie.

"Well, like the kind of mud between his claws," I said. "You can trace all kinds of clues about where a guy or a car or—or a *cat's* been by examining the mud under a microscope."

"My other brother the detective!" said Trina, very sarcastic in tone, paying me back for smiling when Ray called her a dum-dum. "*What* microscope?"

"Well it's too late for that now anyway," said Ray.

But it wasn't all a waste, my mention of such scientific detective work. It did give Ray another good idea.

It came just after supper.

"We may not have a microscope, Angus," he said. "But we do have a micro*phone*."

"Yes, sure," I said, wondering if he was putting me on and wishing he would forget what I said. "But—"

"And we can use that microphone—plus the recorder of course—to conduct some more tests tomorrow."

"Like what?" I said.

"Listen," he said.

Then he told me. And, boy, what a brilliant idea this one is!

I can hardly wait for tomorrow to try it out.

11

THE TRUCK AND THE TABLE

This was Ray's great idea, and this is Ray's voice describing it:

"Why don't we take the recorder out and build up a collection of sounds? I mean all kinds of sounds. Sounds from the town and sounds from the country. We can stop by at Nibs' and Sherry's place and collect some there. Not just horses neighing, which we already have, but horses' hoofbeats, cattle lowing or mooing or whatever it is they do, those bells tinkling. And chickens. Hogs. The sound of a tractor. Milking machines."

"Oh, sure! And birds tweeting and corn growing and worms turning. All those sounds. Say, what *is* this? I thought we were trying to trace the cat's home."

That was Trina. Raising objections. Being very sarcastic.

But Ray wasn't fazed at all. He just ignored her and went on:

"Then in the town we can collect town sounds. Traffic noises. Motor bikes. People in a crowd. Fire bells ringing. Elevator doors maybe. I don't know. Anything. And *then*—"

Here's where he did look at Trina and answer her objections:

"—*then* we come back here and try all those sounds out on the cat. One at a time. Carefully. Studying him carefully. And see what reactions we get."

Even Katie saw the beauty of it then.

"We could find out all kinds of things that way!"

"So what are we waiting for?"

So we went and gathered our sounds.

We had a great time collecting them. Nibs and Sherry thought it was a terrific idea also, and I must say that I don't know how we could have managed without those two kids, especially Nibs. Not only with horses was he good, but he also knew how to make most other animals sound off in a true and genuine way. Sometimes he did it with a word, sometimes with a kind of animal noise of his own, sometimes with a prod of his toe, sometimes with a scratch with the tip of a stick. Inside a couple of hours we'd got on tape, besides horses running and horses neighing, the following:

horses eating hay and stamping;
harness jingling;
buggy wheels rattling, iron on stone;
roosters crowing;
mother hens brooding;
chicks pipe-piping;

hogs grunting;
cows mooing;
their bells tinkling;
a bull bellowing (with Katie squealing with fright in the background);
a goat bleating;
a donkey braying;
and even a bunch of rats squeaking (with both Katie *and* Trina squealing along with them in the background).

This was totally apart from all the mechanical farm sounds, like tractor engines, the milking machines, an electric pump, and Mr. Haywood sharpening some scythes on a stone.

In the town too we had a pretty good time. Being Saturday, it was even busier than a normal day. So as well as the various traffic noises that Ray mentioned—the various engines and so on—we got things like the air brakes on a Greyhound bus, a defective muffler noise (including a beautiful backfire), and all kinds of sounds at a filling station, including the tyre pump. In addition, we got our elevator door noise after all (at the Town Library), which Ray said might be the most important yet, as a back-up to the theory that Amnesia had been living in a city apartment. We also got some pinball machine noises (at a cost of 75 cents), the sound of a lunch counter cash register, a traffic policeman blowing a whistle, a speedboat (though that came out a bit muffled on account it was out in the middle of the river), and a winch.

When we got back to the farmhouse it was after two and we were late for lunch. Trina and Katie and I were all set to skip lunch and start in right away, trying the sounds out on the cat. (We'd had some hot dogs and chocolate milk shakes at the lunch counter—where we also recorded some great mixer sounds, by the way.) But Mom wouldn't hear of it and Ray himself agreed with her, saying it was a job we could not rush.

"Besides," said Mom, "I have news for you. While you were away we made an interesting discovery about the cat ourselves. Right, Clyde?"

Dad nodded. For the first time, he looked really enthusiastic about the Great Inquiry.

"What was it?" asked Trina. "Something useful?"

"Tell us! Tell us!" said Katie.

"While you're eating your lunch," Mom said. "But first—wash up."

It was one of the quickest washing-up and settling-down-to-lunch sessions I've ever known.

Then Mom and Dad told us.

"It was about ten-thirty," said Mom.

"The time doesn't matter," said Dad.

(I said he was enthusiastic, didn't I?)

"Anyway," Mom went on, "everything was very quiet and peaceful with you all out of the house. I was in the kitchen, making bread—"

"And I was in the parlour, writing letters—"

"And the cat was out on the front porch, lying down and looking out over the grass. I know this because just before I started baking I happened to look out and see him, and I called your father's attention to it. Right?"

"Right," Dad said. "He was as relaxed as a cat can be. Save he did have a kind of watchful look, kind of wistful, as if he was looking out for signs of you all coming back."

"Love him!" said Katie, getting off her chair and going to stroke Amnesia where he now lay on his side, near the stove, his eyes nearly closed but his ears pricked, listening to all this.

"Anyway, you can imagine how startled I was only a few minutes later to hear him scratching at the back door—frantically—and then, when I opened it, to see him scurrying in with his body low to the ground and his tail down and his ears back, looking scared to death."

We all stopped eating and drinking.

"What was it?"

"A *bear*?"

"What? What?"

Mom smiled and shook her head.

"I couldn't figure it out at first. He'd made straight for the girls' room and under the bottom bunk, squeezing almost flat to get in that narrow space there. Then I heard it."

"Heard what?"

"Be quiet, Katie, and let Mom get on with her story."

"The truck. It had just swung in around the back and I heard the door slam and men's voices and—you know the sort of sounds."

"To cut a short story even shorter," said Dad, "it was the men with the propane cylinders. They have a regular route, picking up the empty ones and leaving the reserves."

I remembered then that there are always two cylinders out in back: one hooked up to the pipe, providing the gas for present use, with the used empty one next to it, ready to be replaced. That way, nobody ever runs out of fuel in the country.

But what had that got to do with Amnesia?

"My guess is that it was the truck," said Dad. "The heavier engine. He certainly isn't scared of the car."

"Maybe it was the men," said Trina. "Something about *them.*"

"I doubt it," said Mom. "He must have taken fright long before he heard their voices. As soon as the truck turned in off the road is when he must have got up and run."

"Maybe it was a truck he tangled with when he hurt his head," said Ray.

"Yes. Maybe he's been scared of trucks ever since." said Trina.

"We have some truck sounds on tape," I said.

And that reminded the others and they hurried up to finish lunch and get on with the investigation.

Well, let me say right now that it was a very good thing Mom and Dad did have that discovery to tell us about. Because the sound trials we conducted this afternoon, trying all those juicy noises on the cat, were disappointing.

What went wrong, I don't know.

Most of the recordings were good ones.

Some were excellent.

And we did present them properly. There was no rushing through them, the way Katie would have had us do.

"No," said Ray. "We play them back not once, but twice at least. With a good gap between each noise. We don't want to confuse Amnesia. We don't want to bore him, either."

So we set the recorder up on the kitchen table, with the volume turned up nice and clear but not too loud, and the speaker grill turned in the cat's direction. He was lying by the stove still.

There was nothing wrong with the set-up.

It was just that he didn't react much. Not to animal noises or traffic noises. The elevator door sound that we'd been pinning so much of our hopes on just left him cold.

Oh sure, his ears pricked up a little here and there, now and then. But not in the way they had done when Ray had first said the word "amnesia," for instance. There was no sitting up and taking notice. He didn't even lift his head. His eyes did once open very wide for a second or two, I must admit. That was when we played back the squealing rats. But as Ray said:

"Even if his reaction had been stronger there, it wouldn't have told us much. I mean what cat *wouldn't* react to rats?"

Especially disappointing, apart from the elevator no-no, was his reaction to the Greyhound bus sounds.

"You'd think he'd have jumped up at *that*," said Trina. "It sounds so much like a truck. And after what Mom and Daddy discovered this morning—well!"

But there was no reaction at all.

Ray looked thoughtful.

"It seems to prove one thing though."

"What?"

Ray turned to me and looked apologetic.

"Don't get me wrong, Angus. I'm not criticizing your recordings. Some were perfect. Under the circumstances. But maybe to a cat's ears there really is a big difference between a mechanical reproduction, however good, and a natural sound."

I nodded. I'd been thinking just the same thing myself.

"Yeah," I said. "Like with pictures. You show an animal a picture and it means nothing. Just another flat piece of paper. Back home, Sonny Clark showed his dog a brillant picture of a rat one time. Life-size. Perfect. And the mutt just yawned."

Mom came in.

"Any luck? Or do I need to ask, seeing your faces?"

We shook our heads.

"Too bad," she said. "But it's getting late and I need to give this floor a sweep before supper. So you, Ray, and Angus, would you please move the table over to one side?"

Hardly giving it any thought, except to move the recorder safer near the centre of the table, we started to do as she'd asked. We were still very glum, you understand, still very thoughtful, wondering what had gone wrong with our great plan. So we were pretty quiet and slow in our movements, just lifting and moving, Ray forward, me backward.

And why am I telling you all this?

What has all this about a simple job like moving a table got to do with a cat?

Listen.

We had not gone more than three steps when the cat glanced up, saw what we were doing, gave a low growl, went all bristly, and scudded along the floor, belly down, tail down, ears back, and straight into the girls' bedroom and under the bunk.

"Well!" said Mom. "If that wasn't exactly how he behaved this morning!"

"But we didn't make any noise!" I said.

"Is there another truck coming up the road?" wondered Trina, going to the window.

There wasn't.

"It was us," said Ray. "Just the sight of Angus and me, carrying the table. I could swear it."

We talked about it for hours.

Then someone hit on a solution.

Dad.

During supper.

"Well now," he said, putting down his fork, "how about *this* for a theory?"

"What?"

"He behaves twice in one day in exactly the same way but for two different things. *Seemingly* different."

"But they *are* different, Dad!" said Ray, cutting in. "I tell you, we didn't make much noise at all. So where's the link between a noisy truck with a couple of loud-voiced men and Angus and me quietly moving a table from one side of the room to another?"

Dad was grinning. His eyes sparkled behind his glasses.

"Can't you see? You, the great detective? How about you others? Huh? Any of you?"

We shook our heads. Mom looked slightly sore.

"Oh, come on, Clyde! Don't keep us in suspense."

He shook his head, still sparkling.

"I guess these kids of ours have led too sheltered a life, honey. If they had had a father like mine, always on the move from place to place, never settling, never—"

"*Moving men*!"

It was Trina who got it first.

Dad bowed.

"Give that girl a china rabbit!" he said. "First prize! Good thinking, Treen!"

"Of course!" Ray was muttering. "A big truck. Men shouting instructions. Furniture being lifted . . . . Hey! How about that? That could be exactly what happened. A house moving. The cat getting all scared. Running away to hide."

"Or maybe even breaking loose on the journey," said Trina.

"Not dumped at all," I said. "Simply escaping—scared at what it thought was going to happen."

Then Trina slumped.

"But what good does that do us? I mean the truck might have been passing through on the way from—from Hartford, say, to—well—anyplace—New Haven, Stamford—any of those cities."

Ray shook his head.

"Let's not be too sure he jumped from a moving vehicle. If he did, how come he's got no injuries? No recent ones, anyway."

"What then?" I asked.

"Let's look at what's much more likely. A house moving operation, OK. Truck, noise, strange men, furniture being carried around. *That's* when a cat's likely to cut loose. *Before* the actual journey."

"Or after," said Dad. "At the destination. Don't forget that, Ray."

Ray nodded.

"Right! So let's get to work on both those angles, why don't we?"

"I don't get it," said Katie.

"I do," said Trina. "He means for us to inquire if anyone in the neighbourhood, in the town, moved out of a house sometime last Thursday or Friday "

"Correct!" said Ray. "Or *into* a house in the area . . . My guess is *into*. Some newcomer."

"Why?" asked Mom.

"Because I still think Amnesia was an apartment cat, from some big modern building. So that means the move was made *away* from there, *to* here."

So now we have a real hot line of inquiry, something really pinpointed, and tomorrow we're going to follow it right along to the end.

12

NEWS OF A HOME

Today is Monday, and I have good news and bad news.

I will tell you the bad news first.

Our discovery about the truck and the table took place on Saturday, remember. And our theory about the house moving took shape on Saturday night.

So that meant we couldn't get onto our investigation into that angle until yesterday, Sunday. And I specially mention the name of the day because it made a difference.

You see, if it had been a weekday, it would have been all so much easier. The Post Offices in both nearby towns would have been open then, and all we need have done was go and ask there. I mean they're the first ones to know if anyone has moved out of or into the district.

But we couldn't wait.

We had to rush on out and do it the hard way.

I won't tell you about all the inquiries we made yesterday: all the doors we knocked on, all the bells we pushed, all the hopes that were raised at the sight of one empty house, and all the hopes that were dashed when we saw, looking closer, that it obviously had been empty for years.

I won't even tell you about the one house we found, late in the afternoon, on the edge of the second nearest town, where the people *had* just recently moved in, only ten days ago.

It would be too much.

You see, they had a cat. And it had not run away. And it had been quite friendly with the moving men. And anyway it was a black one.

Katie cried, she was so disappointed.

The lady was very sympathetic.

She gave us all a coke and said she'd have taken Amnesia in herself, after hearing us tell about him, only her cat Roger would be very upset. Once, when they had started feeding a stray, Roger had got mad and fought him savagely and so it was goodbye, stray.

Anyway, as I say, it's too painful to go into details like that, especially when they lead nowhere.

Today didn't start much better, either.

First, it was raining again, and a rainy Monday morning in the country isn't much more cheerful than a rainy Monday in the city.

Ray though—I will say this for him—is no slouch.

"If a job's worth doing it's worth being thorough," he said.

So he put on his rain things and biked into both towns to ask at the Post Offices, just to make sure we hadn't missed any recent house movings when we'd inquired the hard way.

We hadn't. Which made it all the worse somehow, at the thought of all that wasted effort!

Dad was a bit scornful when Ray came back with his sad news.

"Why didn't you simply bike to the Haywood farm and telephone the Post Offices?"

"Because if there had been news of a recent move I wanted to be ready to follow it up right away."

Just like Ray, that. He'd have loved to have been able to come back with everything all sewn up and Amnesia's owner traced.

Much of the rest of today we just sat around and played board games or read or just waited. You know. Waited for the rain to stop, or for someone to drop by and say they knew where the cat had come from—someone who'd been alerted by our earlier inquiries.

No one did.

The rain wasn't in any hurry to stop, either.

Mom did make another discovery, but it was only a minor one.

"Have you noticed how he's started to leave his milk?" she asked. "At first I thought he'd gone off milk altogether. I'd pick it up and pour it down the sink when it had been standing a day. But yesterday I forgot, and there it is, and just look at him."

We *were* just looking at him!

Amnesia was really enjoying that saucer of milk. He was crouched right over it, with his tail curled around his back legs and his shoulders hunched.

"Yik!" said Trina, over the top of her book.

"It's all yellow and solid round the edges," said Katie, bending down at the cat's side. "It's sour!"

"But he seems to prefer it that way," said Mom.

Well, you couldn't deduce much from that. Nothing that seemed to make sense, anyway.

I suppose that's how we started inventing nonsense theories.

Like Ray's, about the milk:

"I guess his owners must belong to a strange religious sect who won't eat or drink anything until it's going bad."

Or like Trina's, about the crack in his head:

"Talking of strange religious sects, how about him being a space cat? How about him being landed from a UFO in all that thunder and lightning, just to spy on us earthlings? That crack, you know, could be a wire. He could be controlled by someone in Mars right now."

"Yeah, maybe in Mars that's how they have their milk, nearly solid," said Ray. "All those long space voyages, too, when they can never get fresh milk."

"Or maybe it's not a control wire, but some sort of bugging device," I said. "Maybe it's not from Mars at all. Just some foreign power that dropped him here by mistake, thinking it was the Pentagon."

Well, we had to try to keep our spirits up *somehow*.

Oh yes—and around that part of the day, when we were just kidding around, we made another small discovery.

It was when the cat got up and walked away from us and to the door. (We were in the parlour.)

"Now we've offended him with all this crazy talk," said Trina. "He wants out."

"I don't blame him," murmured Katie, going to help him.

"No, let him open it himself," said Ray. "Cats are good at that."

The door was just a little way ajar, not quite wide enough for Amnesia to squeeze through.

"Go on, pal!" said Ray, when the cat turned his head and gave a small mew, asking for assistance. "Pull it open."

Sure enough, the cat turned and lifted a paw.

But—*not* sure enough—it simply prodded and dabbed at it, then scratched slightly, then tapped, instead of hooking his paw around the edge and pulling.

"Well I'll be darned!" said Ray. "That's the first cat I ever saw who doesn't know how to open a door wider when it's already part way open!"

Katie said we were cruel keeping Amnesia waiting like this, and she went on and opened it.

We kicked around a few possible reasons for that peculiarity but didn't get very far.

Trina said he might have got a thorn in his paw or a cut or something, which sent Katie hurrying after the cat to make sure. But he hadn't.

Ray said it might be something connected with his old head injury—the brain damage theory again.

Katie looked as if she might object, but it didn't develop into anything because just then Mom came in with the good news I mentioned earlier.

Well, *fairly* good news anyway.

"I think I've found him a home," she announced.

We stared at her. She had just come back from marketing in town. She was still carrying a sack of groceries, so eager was she to tell her news, and we all let her stand there holding them, so stunned were we by what she had said.

"You—you mean—?"

Ray was stuttering—very unusual for him.

We others were still speechless.

"Now don't get me wrong," Mom said quickly. "I don't mean his real home. I just said *a* home. But since it looks as if we'll never trace his real owners, this is good enough surely. At least it means he'll *live*. He won't have to be put to sleep or anything when we leave."

"But—*where*, Mom?"

Trina's book had slid out of her hands and onto the floor without her even noticing it.

"At your friends the Haywoods. Wonderful people. I stopped by to get some cream and butter and it was Mrs. Haywood who suggested the idea. She said there was plenty of room on their farm for an extra cat and he'd be welcome any time."

So there it is.

The fairly good news.

And the reason I say "fairly" good is because somehow it isn't the same as if we'd found his real home.

But Mom is right.

Better this way than losing his life.

So, late this afternoon, we took him in a good big duffel bag, with an old sweater of Katie's to lie on, in the car, to the Haywoods, and he *was* welcomed.

Nibs and Sherry had fixed him a nice dry place in the attic in the farmhouse, with a box of dirt, and some dishes of food, and they're going to keep him in there a day or two until he gets used to them. Then they'll let him roam around the rest of the house.

"May we come and play with him?" said Katie.

"Well, not for a couple of days, honey," said Mrs. Haywood. "It's best if he settles here first."

Katie gave a big swallow, then nodded.

She's really pretty sensible for her age.

But it's going to be hard for her, I know.

And not just for her.

But still and all . . . .

I'll make another report in a day or so, just to round it all off.

As Ray says:

"Just so long as he *does* settle, OK. Just so long as he doesn't run away from *there*. We don't want a missing cat search as well as a missing home search on our hands!"

13

THE MYSTERY OF THE DOORS

Now guess what!

No. Wait.

Let's take this nice and calmly.

Listen . . .

Today is Thursday.

On Monday, when the cat had been taken to the Haywood farm, I said that I would be making further reports about how he was settling in and so on.

Well, Tuesday and Wednesday, I guess I didn't have much heart. Somehow we all got to miss that cat more than we'd expected. Even Dad had to admit that the place didn't seem quite the same without him, and once more we began to get that feeling that there was something wrong with a farm without any tame animals at all.

Besides, over at the other farm, the real farm, the cat's new farm, there wasn't much to report. As Mrs.

Haywood had said, the plan was to keep him secure in that attic room for a few days so that he would settle in better, and they stuck to that plan even though Nibs was impatient to introduce him to the other cats and generally show him around his new home.

There was one slight change in plan, though.

If you remember, Katie asked if she could visit with Amnesia and Mrs. Haywood said, No, not for a few days—again so that he would settle in easier.

Well, Katie really meant actually visit with him in the attic, of course, so she could hug him and nuzzle him and generally slobber over him. But later Mrs. Haywood said she'd have no objection to our visiting the farm in the ordinary way, just so long as we didn't go into the attic or anywhere near it.

All right. So on both Tuesday and yesterday we went to the Haywood farm, right after breakfast, just to find out how the cat was doing, and I for one was pleased to hear that he was settling down, even though he wasn't eating much, which was only to be expected.

"Have you tried him with sour milk?" said Katie yesterday, in a very high voice, which goes like that when she's excited or anxious.

"Shush, honey, or he'll hear you!" said Mrs. Haywood softly, going and shutting the door. (We were in their kitchen and the door led out into the hall and stairs.)

So Katie shushed, and put her hand to her mouth, and rolled her eyes.

But as soon as we were outside and on our way home again, up went her voice once more, wondering if Amnesia missed her, and whether he was still sleeping on her old sweater, and if they were changing the dirt in his tray often enough—so that Nibs got a bit mad and asked her if she thought they didn't know how to look after animals at their place, or *what*!

I didn't think much of this at the time, as they argued and yacked and snapped at each other all the way to the road. But *now*, well, I wonder.

Attics have windows, and sounds travel through them fairly easily. . . .

Anyway, as I say, those last two days I didn't have much heart or interest to make a report, because without Amnesia and his problem we went back to doing mainly holiday things.

Like one day we all drove out to a place called Gillette Castle, which is on a hill but isn't really a castle. It's where an actor lived who played the part of Sherlock Holmes, the greatest detective of all, and where everything in it is made of wood, even the light switches.

And like crossing the river by ferry.

And like yesterday driving up to Mystic to see the whaling museum.

Dad and Mom were trying really hard, I think, to take our minds off the cat as much as possible. Maybe they'd have succeeded, too, because they had another trip planned for today to take us up to an old village called Sturbridge where everyone living there dresses up old-fashioned.

But *then* . . .

Listen . . .

This morning. Before breakfast. Mom was first up, getting things ready in the kitchen, as usual. Dad was still in bed, as usual. And Ray and I were next up, getting our washing-up water, *not* as usual.

I mean it was not usual for us to be out there before the girls.

"I wonder what's wrong with them this morning?" said Mom, glancing over at the door of their room. "I keep hearing them moving about, and whispering. They were doing it when I first came in here fifteen minutes ago.

Ray just shrugged as if to say who could tell what girls would be doing next, and who cared.

But I listened, always interested in sounds and tones and things like that, and—sure enough—they were still whispering, very excitedly, then fizzing—you know—that nervous giggly noise.

"Sounds like they're thinking of playing some trick," I said. "It's—"

But I didn't get any further because that's when their door was flung open and there they were.

All *three* of them!

"Good heavens!" gasped Mom.

"What—where—?" Again Ray had got the stammers.

And again I was speechless, just staring.

I'll never forget those three faces: the two girls and the cat they were holding up between them.

I've already said how different Katie's face is to Trina's: one fair and toothy, and the other dark and all eyes.

And I don't need to say that there isn't usually much resemblance between a cat's face and a kid's.

But this time there was. There was something very very similar about *those* three faces: Katie's, Trina's, and Amnesia's.

Something to do with the expression, I guess.

Pleased. Very pleased indeed. But also anxious, scared of what might happen next, scared of what people might say about the reason they were so pleased.

"He came back!" whispered Katie, unable to control

her smile, those big teeth just bursting out of her lips.

"He came back in the night!" murmured Trina, *her* mouth a bit defiant now, bottom lip out, but smiling all the same, and with very shiny eyes.

"Neeyip!" whispered the cat, as if agreeing, but very politely, very apologetic.

"He tapped on the window."

"I knew it was him."

"So we let him in. Rather than upset everyone in the middle of the night," said Trina.

"*Great! Just great!*" boomed another voice.

Dad's.

He was there in his bathrobe and his expression was just the opposite of his words. Most mornings, first thing, without his glasses, his face has that strained worried look. But now it was worse. He looked sick.

"He must have escaped," said Trina.

"Maybe Nibs didn't shut the door properly," said Katie. "Thinks he's so smart about animals and didn't think to shut the door!" she jeered.

"Isn't it wonderful, though, how cats can find their way about?" said Trina.

But neither Dad nor Mom were in any mood to be talked off the main point, which was this:

"Now he'll *never* settle at the Haywood farm!"

Mom agreed.

"I'm afraid you're right, Clyde. And after Saturday, when we're not here—"

"Besides, it wouldn't be fair to the Haywoods."

We were all looking—kids and cat—at the two grown-ups, from one worried face to the other. At least four of us knew what was coming next, and I'm not sure that the fifth didn't sense it, either.

"It looks as if we're back to Square One," said Dad.

"Only now there are only two days left," sighed Mom.

"Well all right then," said Ray, speaking up at last. "So we continue our investigations."

"We'll find this cat's owner," I said, backing him up, "or—or—"

I was going to say something ordinary like "or bust"—or "die in the attempt"—when it occurred to me that Amnesia was the one who would die if we failed.

"I shall make a vow," said Trina, very loud, but with her voice wobbling all over the place. "*I vow that I will never read another book if we don't find Amnesia's owner!*"

That was a terrible vow for her.

"And—and I'll never eat any breakfast, ever!" said Katie, which, considering the trouble Mom has to get her to eat any anyway, wasn't such a big deal.

But the kid meant it that way. Tears were pouring down her cheeks.

"Talking of breakfast," Ray said, "may we get right on with it?.We have work to do and we can't affort to waste another second."

He was right.

And as soon as we were through with the meal, he ordered us into the parlour.

"The recorder, Angus," he said. "One more time. I want you to play it all back. All your reports. And you others, I want you to keep quiet and listen. Hard. I want to make sure we missed nothing. Not a single possible clue."

So we did.

We listened harder than we've ever listened to anything, while Katie hugged the cat and dried her cheeks on the fur over his head and neck.

And that's how Trina got this great idea.

"Stop!" she said. "Right there!"

I stopped the tape.

"Now play that bit back. From where the cat gets up and goes to the door and I say we must have offended him."

I clicked the fast rewind, stopped it, switched on the playback, almost exactly where she said.

Then we listened again to how the cat had been unable to open the door.

"Right!" said Trina. "That's the best clue yet!"

Ray was frowning.

"Go on. . . . Why?"

"Because," said my sister, the Second Greatest Detective of All, "it just doesn't make sense that an intelligent and healthy cat like this shouldn't know a trick like that. Unless one thing."

"What?"

"Unless it has just never been used to doors."

Ray frowned harder.

"But that's dumb!" he said. "He isn't a wild cat. He isn't a new-born kitten. He's fully grown and he's lived in a home, a good home, most of his life. That's obvious."

"So?"

Trina was flushed with triumph still, completely unput-down.

"So show me a home without doors."

"All right," said Trina, getting up. "Let's go."

"But where?"

"To show you just that kind of a home. Oh, sure, it's got doors of a kind. But not this kind, on hinges, that a cat can pull or push open."

"Wait a minute," I said. "Do you mean—?"

"I mean *sliding* doors!" said Trina. "And what sort of a home has all sliding doors, to save space? I'll tell you. A *trailer*!"

14

THE CAT AND THE WOMAN

Suddenly we saw what Trina had in mind. Suddenly we realized why she was so excited and eager to get moving.

"You mean the trailer over by the creek?" said Ray.

She nodded rapidly.

"The one that Nibs and Sherry showed us. Yes. So—"

"Just a minute, though," I said, remembering something else. "The woman wasn't home when they took us to look at it."

"No," said Trina. "But that doesn't mean to say she isn't back *now*! Oh, look, come *on*! We're wasting time."

Ray agreed.

"But hold it just one more second," he said. "Just to make sure we don't waste any more time, why don't we take Amnesia along with us?"

"No!" said Katie. "He's tired. He had a long journey in the dark last night and—"

"Be quiet, Katie!" said Trina. She turned to Ray. "I don't get it," she said. "*Why* take him along?"

Ray grinned. I guess he'd been feeling a bit miffed at not thinking of the trailer idea himself, but now he was getting into his stride again, taking control.

"Why, to see how he *himself* reacts when he sees the place! Then even if the woman hasn't come back yet we'll get a pretty good idea if he did live there."

"Oh, yes! Sure! Great!" said Trina. "Katie, get the duffel bag, please."

Katie ran off to find it, just as enthusiastic about taking the cat as the rest of us now.

"And another thing," said Ray, when she'd come back with the bag and Trina was holding it open and Katie was lowering a very limp, very sleepy-eyed Amnesia into it. "Even if it turns out that he didn't live in that particular trailer, his reaction should tell us whether we're on the right track or not. Whether he did in fact live in *a* trailer. Then we can go ahead and concentrate on other trailers in the area."

We all agreed that this was pretty good thinking too.

All except the cat, that is.

He didn't struggle, even when we'd pulled the zipper of the bag to within an inch or two of the end, leaving the last bit for air. But you could tell somehow that he wasn't wildly crazy about going into that bag again.

"He thinks we're taking him back to the Haywood farm!" said Katie. Then she stuck her mouth near the zipper hole. "Well we're not then, honey!" she murmured softly. "We're taking him back to his real home."

The cat gave back a soft pitiful mew in reply.

Mom and Dad had already gone out with the car.

They were going into town to buy presents to take home with us, saying they'd also be stopping by at the Haywood farm to tell them what had happened. So we had to fix the duffel bag onto Ray's bike, slinging it over the handlebars.

This didn't cheer the cat up any.

Before we'd even reached the road, he'd set up a kind of moaning—low and hopeless and lost and sad.

"Honestly, you'd think we were taking him to the ASPCA already!" said Trina.

"He's scared!" said Katie. "Oh, stop and let me carry him! I don't mind the walk."

"No," said Ray. "It would take too long. And he still wouldn't like it."

"He's right, honey," Trina told her.

After that, Katie just nibbled her bottom lip with those big teeth of hers, but didn't make any more protest. Even the cat quieted some, and only gave out his moans when we turned sharply, like from the road to the farm road, and from the farm road to the narrower one leading to the creek.

"I think he can *sense* he's getting nearer home," said Trina hopefully, as we approached the trees near the creek.

I doubted that. Remembering last night, I'd got the feeling that the cat was busy inside the bag sensing which direction we were taking him, like making some sort of radar chart inside that stripey head of his. I also began to imagine that those moans when we made sudden turns weren't so much signs of despair pure and simple, but of a mixture of despair and annoyance at having to make yet another adjustment to the radar course he was plotting.

Anyway, it soon seemed worth all the discomfort he was having to put up with.

"Look!" said Trina, as we took the last corner through the trees and Amnesia gave his last moan, and we pulled up. "She's back."

We could now see the trailer on its grassy platform, clear of the trees, and, sure enough, there was a blue car parked next to it.

Also the door of the trailer was partly open.

"Yeah!" said Ray, suddenly sounding a bit doubtful. "So it seems. But just take a look at that door."

I saw at once what he meant.

Hinges.

"*That* isn't a sliding door," he said.

And now his voice had that Strike One tone.

Trina isn't as easily put off.

"Yes, but all the doors inside will be sliding ones," she said. "Bound to be."

"OK!" sighed Ray. "But—"

"Oh, give me the bag and be quiet!"

Well, Ray didn't object. He knew as well as I that there's no stopping Trina in this mood. Also, of course, there was the fact that he leaves all the first talking to her, and that if he raised one peep of an objection more she'd be likely to tell him to go and begin the inquiring himself.

There were some steps in front of the door—two or three—I forget. But Trina took them in one stride, the bag in her arms and Katie right behind her. I just didn't have time to get the recorder ready and in the right position, but I guess maybe it was as well. Because what happened next could very easily have bust some delicate part inside, I'm certain.

Knock-knock! goes Trina, very confident now, already with one hand moving toward the zipper to open it wider.

"Yes?" says the woman who comes to the door, quite pleasantly, quite a pleasant-looking woman, not very big, dressed in one of those light safari suits, with big sunglasses and a blue scarf in her hair.

"We were wondering, ma'am, if you've lost a—"

And that's where my recorder would surely have blown a tube or something.

Because before Trina even had time to say the word "cat," Amnesia's big round head had jerked up through the wider hole she had made, and the woman let out one horrible high-pitched gargling kind of a scream.

Katie just turned and ran to where Ray was straddling his bike and gaping.

Amnesia's head disappeared, ears flat as he went down into the bag, and who could blame him?

And the woman went on screaming for about half a minute longer, just plain hysterical, her hands up to her face, her glasses knocked half off her nose, and even her hair and her scarf somehow falling loose.

Trina stood her ground more from shock than bravery, as she was the first to admit later.

"Ma'am!" I heard her say, as the screaming died down a little into a kind of terrible gulping and gasping. "Is something—?"

Then the woman stepped back and slammed the door. I heard a bolt go.

Trina turned and looked at us, white-faced. We shook our heads. We couldn't understand it either. We were still too shocked to speak anyway, even if we'd had any ideas.

Then Trina turned back to the door and knocked again. As she told us afterward:

"It wasn't that I was being persistent about the cat still. I guess I'd forgotten about him for the moment. I just wanted to know what was wrong and if we could help."

So:

"Ma'am," she began, putting her mouth close to the edge of the door, "if there's something we can—"

"You can take—that—that cat—away! Now! *Now!* NOW!!"

It was a horrible sound. Gaspy and jerky and strangled at first (so that I began to wonder if there wasn't someone in there with her, with his hands tight around her throat)—but then rising into the scream again.

"Come on, Treen!" said Ray. "Right now!"

"Well!" said Trina, handing over the bag to him. "Well would you believe!"

"That woman sounds crazy," I said.

"You can say that again," murmured Ray.

"But—but she seemed all right at first!" said Trina. "Not until—"

"Trina," said Ray, "pick up your bike and *move*! We can talk about it later. Right now I think we should get as far away as possible. People who act like that can be dangerous, no matter what triggers it off."

Katie was already on her way.

There came a violent bumping noise from the trailer.

We others didn't need telling again.

15

THE SPLIT

So we took the cat back home.

We didn't say much on the way back and we didn't say much when we got there, either. Not at first.

This was because we'd no sooner let the cat out of the bag than Mom and Dad came driving up.

"Er—maybe we'd better keep quiet about what happened," said Ray.

We others just nodded, to show we agreed.

I don't think Ray himself knew why we should say nothing about the trip to the trailer. It was just one of those things and we all felt the same way about it. You know how it is. Something strange or terrible happens and somehow you just don't feel like telling your parents about it right away. It is almost as if you feel guilty—as if it was your fault that whatever has happened has happened. You feel kind of embarrassed, as if—well, you *know*.

So we listened to what Mom and Dad had to say about the Haywoods, and how Mr. and Mrs. Haywood agreed that it wouldn't be much use taking Amnesia back now, and how Nibs and Sherry were mad at us, thinking we'd snuck out in the night and blown whistles or something to entice that cat out of the house, but how they'd soon get over it. And we just nodded and said "Oh, yes?" or "Oh, no?" or "Sure!"

Then they showed us the presents they'd got for people back in Philadelphia, and we were polite about them, too, and showed some interest, but all the time—I'll tell you—we were just *busting* to go someplace quiet and talk about the woman and the trailer and decide what it was with her and the cat.

Anyway, finally we did.

Ray said he thought he'd seen another black snake in back of the old horse barn and wondered if we'd like to take a look. Katie thought he really meant it and refused straight out, saying she'd rather stay on the porch with the cat. We didn't argue because, as Trina said as soon as we were around the other side of the barn:

"This is no business for little kids."

"Oh?" said Ray. "*You're* realizing that too, are you?"

Trina said yes, very firmly—but it soon came out that her idea of why it wasn't kid stuff didn't match up with Ray's.

Ray's was simply a kind of grown-up idea—sensible, yes, but just dull and responsible.

"The poor woman's mentally unbalanced. Obviously. Probably that's why she lives alone like that, kind of like a hermit. So we just keep away."

"Well I don't agree!" said Trina. "Mentally unbalanced, sure. I'll go along with you there. But *why*? Why does she hide herself away there? And why did she suddenly go like that when she saw Amnesia?"

"How should I know?" said Ray. "Maybe she just doesn't like cats."

"No. There was something more than that. Right, Angus?"

I had to agree with her.

"Looked like it to me," I said.

Maybe I shouldn't have.

If there's one thing that gets my brother good and sore it is when he's in the minority. Especially when I—his only brother—take sides with the opposition. He gets all clammed up then. Mad, but cold. Hurt, but independent.

"You read too many dumb books," he said to Trina, not even glancing at me. "That's your trouble. Also you can't ever admit your mistakes."

"What mistakes?"

"Like finding out the trailer did have a door on hinges, after all."

"But I *told* you about that. I said I bet there were sliding doors inside, and I still think so. But even if they weren't, we were still on the right track, going there. That woman *knew* Amnesia!"

Trina said this last bit in such a doomlike kind of voice that Ray had to smile.

"There you go! Dramatizing again! Books—too many books!"

Trina took no notice. She turned to me.

"Didn't you get that feeling, Angus? Sure you did! We were right up there, near her, weren't we? Not chickening out somewhere in the background."

"Hey, now—!" began Ray.

But Trina was in orbit, her eyes wide and serious.
"And you know what I think, Angus? I think a terrible crime was committed in that trailer. And I think that it involved the woman and Amnesia both!"

"Oh, boy!" groaned Ray. "When does the second feature start?"

"Crime?" I said, staring at Trina. "Huh—what kind of a crime?"

"I'm not sure," she said. "I was trying to piece things together while Mom was yacking about those gifts. Trying to fit in moving men and trucks and so on. One time I thought it might be a big robbery, a hi-jacking or something."

"Too many books!" jeered Ray. "Too much television!"

But I noticed he was still hanging around, as keen to hear the rest of Trina's theory as I was.

"*How* a hi-jacking?" I said.

"Well, like this. A truck gets held up and hi-jacked on the Turnpike, say. Now even at night it wouldn't be safe to off-load it on the spot. So what do they do? They bring it someplace quiet. Someplace like this. Then they off-load into the trailer—the perfect place for hiding the stuff till its cooler."

"Hiding what, for Pete's sake?" sneered Ray. "Bullion from Fort Knox? Another consignment of crisp new one-hundred-dollar bills for the First National Bank?"

Trina shrugged.

"Who knows? Something valuable, anyway. And something bulky, too—bulky enough to need two men to lift and carry."

"Oh!" I said. "You mean like moving men?"

Ray couldn't stand it any longer.

"Angus, Angus!" he howled. "Don't tell me you're *believing* this garbage?"

"And so," said Trina, still ignoring him, "you'd have the situation on the night of the storm, with strange men tromping in and out of the trailer, scaring the cat, causing him to—"

"Right!" said Ray. "Stop right there! Hold it and I'll prove you're wrong." He turned to me. "Night of the storm, Angus. Lots of rain. Ground all wet and muddy. Now. Did *you* see any deep tracks that looked like being made by a truck? Huh? Did you? Either today or nearer the time, when we went with Nibs and Sherry? Because sure as heck *I* didn't!"

But Trina was smiling. Sweetly.

"I said it was only a *theory*, didn't I?" Then her face darkened. "But it was something of the sort, some *truly* bad crime, I'm sure. And you know what I really think now, Angus?"

I shook my head.

"That it was worse even than that. I think there might have been a *murder* in that trailer!"

"A—a murder?"

"Oh, I'm going!" said Ray. "This is too much!"

But I noticed he was staying right where he was.

"Yes, a murder," said Trina. "I think the cat's true owner lived in that trailer. Maybe—no, *probably*—another woman. And this second woman, for some reason, came along and murdered her. You *yourself* said she looked dangerous!" said Trina, turning on Ray.

"Yes, but—but—"

"They might even have been friends, Angus. This one might just have come as a house guest. But then they had a fight. Perhaps drinking. Perhaps that and the storm made this woman very uptight, jumpy, *homicidal*. So she killed her friend, in front of the cat's very eyes. And when she came to lift the body and drag it out to bury it under the trees or dump it in the creek, weighted down, the cat escaped. And now. . . ."

Trina's voice had gone low. We could hear things in the background: a blue jay, a car in the distance, the rattle of plates from the kitchen, Dad's voice saying something to Katie on the porch. But I for one felt as shivery as if it was a moonless midnight with only the sound of night birds, as Trina murmured on:

". . . when she sees the cat, it all comes back. It's like Amnesia had come back to accuse her and she breaks down totally."

Ray took a deep breath.

"Thank you, Edgar Allen Poe! And now that the Creature Feature is over, Angus, here is a message from the sponsor. How about snapping out of this trance and remembering there is work to do? I suggest that right after lunch we start inquiring at all the trailers and trailer camps in the area, systematically, working outward."

It didn't occur to me then that here was a guy who'd just been saying that trailers didn't all have sliding doors and that Trina had been mistaken.

Trina missed it too. But she was still deep in her theory.

"I say we concentrate on *this* trailer. I say we go and keep that place under observation. There's plenty of cover. See what the woman does when she thinks she's alone and she's gotten over the shock."

"I tell you she could be *dangerous*!" said Ray.

"You bet she could be!" said Trina.

"I mean quite apart from your crazy theory. . . . So

why don't we drop it? Angus, why don't we work out an itinerary right now?"

"Angus," said Trina, "please stay with me. I—I don't mind admitting I don't want to go there alone. And I couldn't get Katie into something like that—"

"No! She's more sense!" jeered Ray.

"But I *will* go alone!" said Trina to me, her lip jutting. "I'll go back there on my own if you refuse."

"If you do go back there," said Ray, "either of you, or both, I'll—"

He stopped.

I knew what he'd been going to say, and I knew why he'd stopped.

He'd been going to say:

"I'll tell Dad and Mom and they'll stop you."

But with us three older kids it would have been going against the Unwritten Law. With us three older kids, finking is *out*. O-U-T.

He sighed.

"OK, Angus," he said. "I guess I can get around the trailers just as quickly on my own. You go with this dumb girl and see she comes to no harm. Just for the rest of this day, mind. Because if the owners aren't traced tomorrow, our last full day, if the owners aren't traced then, alive *or* dead—it's curtains for the cat."

Trina blinked. That kind of language—*curtains for the cat*—book language—always gets through to her.

"That suits me," she said.

"All right then," said Ray, now in a position to take charge again. "So remember. *One*—no taking Katie with you—"

"Are you kidding!" said Trina.

"And *Two*—no direct confrontations. Whatever that

woman does, you keep well back and out of sight, OK? Anything unusual you report to me when you get back."

We said we would do that.

"All right, then," he said. "But I still say you'll be wasting your time."

"That's what he thinks!" murmured Trina, as we made our way back to the house.

16

STAKE-OUT

It was one of those clear, still afternoons, when sounds travel a long distance. Even very small sounds.

So Trina and I were doubly pleased that we hadn't taken Katie with us, as we biked along the dirt road in the direction of the creek, close together, side by side, so that we could keep our voices down to whispers.

Of course, while we were travelling over the field part of the route, between corn and grass, we were very exposed to *sight*. I mean if the Strange Lady of the Trailer (that was the way we'd come to think of her and speak of her as we made our plans after lunch)—if she'd taken it into her head to come driving along the track right then, there wouldn't have been much we could do to avoid being seen by her. We could have dove into the corn, I suppose, bikes and all, but before then she would have been bound to spot us—as we travelled heads and shoulders above the growing stuff.

"Still," (as Trina had said), "if she does drive off in her

car before we get there, there won't be much point in carrying on with our stake-out. She won't be around to *be* observed. And we'll just have to try later is all."

Anyway, nothing like that happened. Everywhere else things were moving, sure. High in the sky a jet droned. Somewhere on the farm a tractor coughed into life. A motorbike rasped away over toward the highway. And there came a heavy chug-chugging from just beyond where we were heading—but not a car engine, something much heavier, some kind of river boat, I guessed.

On the dirt road itself nothing moved except our two bikes, and they made only the slightest ticking, not even as loud as some of the insects in the grass.

Then even that stopped when we got to the first trees, and we dismounted, and lifted the bikes the last few feet, and placed them in a hollow, screened by the low branches of some saplings.

"Ready for a quick getaway," Trina had said, when we made our plans.

"I hope we can find someplace suitable," had been my comment—knowing how big a gap there is sometimes between what Trina *plans* and what is actually *possible*.

Well, this time she had been on-target.

As I stood up after placing the bike there, I gave her the "just fine" sign with my finger and thumb in a circle, and she nodded as if to say, "How else could it have been?"

Then, going back to the road as it wound through the trees—but keeping close to the edge, where it was grassy—we continued on foot.

This was Trina's idea also.

"If we go through the trees for the last hundred feet,

there's a chance we might stumble into holes, or trip over old fallen branches or stumps, or get stuck in bogs," she had said.

But glancing around me right then, on the spot, I could see she'd made a mistake. Just a glance told me she hadn't remembered that part of the place correctly, because except for saplings there wasn't much undergrowth—not enough to cause you to trip over old stumps or stumble into holes. The ground was pretty level, anyway.

But also I could see something else, and it reminded me how you can often do the right thing even by mistake. Because although there were none of the dangers Trina had imagined, there was one that was just as bad. Lots of dry twigs. A foot pressed down on any one of them could have made quite a crack.

And in this stillness it would sound like a gun.

Why, even already, we could hear the rattle of a cup and saucer or something similar, and a spoon, coming from the clearing. Even before we got to where we could see, these sounds told us the woman was home.

This was good to know.

Two or three seconds later it was good to know she *was* actually in her trailer, too, because just then, somewhere over in the trees behind us and to our left, a twig did crack.

We stopped and listened.

Silence.

Then more cup-and-saucer rattling from ahead.

So it couldn't be her.

Trina shrugged and put her mouth close to my ear. "A squirrel, maybe?"

I nodded. It hadn't been all that big a crack—I mean like a pistol shot.

"Something of the kind," I whispered.

But it made us glad that we ourselves were treading on soft grass as we proceeded.

When we got our first glimpse of the trailer and car—cream glints and blue glints, through the trees—just before the final bend, we stopped again and stepped back and began to look around.

This was going to be a very tricky part of the operation. This time we *would* have to step among the trees. We would have to do it in order to find a suitable hiding place which would still give us a clear view of the trailer.

Well, once more we were in luck.

Trina tapped my arm and pointed.

Between the trunks of the trees, I could see some bushes, and these bushes were closer to the trailer, near the very edge of the clearing.

Slowly, taking a step, pausing, looking; taking another step, pausing, looking; *listening*; taking another step—and so on—we got to the bushes.

"Perfect!" whispered Trina, tickling my ear.

She was right.

It was.

Through the leaves of the bush we had a perfect view of the trailer. Its door was ajar again, and behind the window near it, which had a filmy sort of curtain, we could see shadowy movements that seemed to fit in with the rattling.

"Doing the dishes?" whispered Trina.

I nodded.

"Probably."

I was still busy observing, noticing the car was there, where it had been earlier, and noticing that this time the hood was pointed away from the road.

That was important to me just then.

I was beginning to feel very nervous, you see.

Now that we were actually *there*, and we could even hear her, even see her, even though it was only her shadow, I began to remember in every detail how she'd looked when she'd seen the cat. I remembered how she'd yelled. I remembered all the theories Trina had been talking about. And suddenly those theories didn't seem all that crazy, and I began to wonder what had gotten into us, just a couple of kids, to take such a risk, and I tell you: I was pretty glad to note the direction that car was pointing.

At least it would give us time to get to the bikes in an emergency, while she got it turned around.

Yet even then—how long would it be before she caught us up? I mean might it be safer to abandon the bikes and just run? Like through the corn, where she couldn't follow with the car?

Then I forced myself to relax some, as we crouched in a more comfortable position, and I rubbed my fingers around the edges of my recorder, which seemed to help—you know—being something very familiar and friendly.

About the recorder, by the way . . .

What we hoped to record, I just don't know.

Trina had said:

"Maybe you'll get something incriminating. Something that will prove what happened on the night of the storm."

But I don't think even my imaginative sister really thought that.

I think her idea was really more in line with leaving a Last Message.

She pretended it was a joke, back home, before we'd started.

"Just to test the recorder, to show that it's in working order, why don't we—"

I'd cut in there.

"It *is* in working order. No need to test it."

"No, but just in case. Just let me say something."

So I'd shrugged and let her.

And this is what she had said, winking at me as if it was all a great joke:

"In case something happens to us and we are no longer seen any more and only this instrument is found, we, Katrina Mary Bleeker and Angus Westlake Bleeker, were on a mission. This mission was keeping observation this afternoon, Thursday the thirteenth, on the Strange Lady of the Trailer. Our brother, Raymond Anthony Bleeker, will tell you where and who and why."

Well, like I said, it suddenly didn't seem all that big a joke, but at least it was a consolation.

Anyway, enough about that.

Here's what actually happened.

We crouched and we watched.

We stood and we watched.

We kneeled and we watched.

We sat and we watched.

We lay down and we watched.

We half-kneeled and half-lay and we watched.

Then we went through all the positions again, with variations.

For *hours*!

Oh, boy—I tell you—the next time I see a stake-out in a TV police thing, I won't wish I was there with them, joining in, sharing the excitement. No, sir. Because stake-outs are only exciting when they don't last for hours. Of course, even stake-outs on television are supposed to last hours sometimes, but there they have directors to cut it short and show you only the thrilling bits. I sure wish we'd had a director, this afternoon.

Mind you, it would have been great if we'd really been there to make nature recordings. Especially of bugs. That would have been really *fascinating*. All those chirpings, buzzings, hummings, clickings, whinings, creakings, tickings. And not just sound recordings of insects, either. Think of the *flesh* recordings to go with them. I mean the ones we actually did collect, on our arms and wrists, our legs, our necks, oh, all over!

In fact I was thinking about this—thinking what a great show we could have given our friends in Philly. Like:

"Now you see this scar here, and this red patch here, and this row of prick-marks here. . . . Well, they were made by bugs that sounded like this. . . . and this . . . and this."

I was thinking about this, I say, and also about tapping Trina on the shoulder and giving her the Let's Go nod, when we got action at last.

Instead of me tapping her shoulder, she gripped mine.

"Look!" she whispered. "She's coming out."

I looked. I saw the door swing open wider, and the woman's arm on the inside handle.

Then she seemed to hesitate.

But not for long.

She had been reaching for something just inside the trailer, something that must have been propped in a corner there.

Then she had it, and then she stepped out with it.

A spade!

Well then I forgot all my stings and itches and cramps and stiffnesses. Instead, every muscle and every inch of my skin began to tingle.

"Where's she going with *that*?" whispered Trina.

The answer was:

"Behind the trailer and into the trees that side."

But I couldn't get my tongue and teeth to work.

My mouth was too dry.

I was thinking of Trina's murder theory again.

Had we got the woman so worried this morning that she'd decided to dig something up and move it to a better hiding place?

"Listen!"

Trina again.

I listened.

At first I thought it was my heart thudding.

Then I realized it was the sound of a spade, slicing into fairly soft but solid earth.

"We have to get closer!" whispered Trina. "See what she's digging up."

The thudding continued.

I tried to judge the distance across the clearing from where we were.

About fifty feet to the trailer itself, I reckoned. Then around it and into the trees over there, say another fifteen.

Too wide, too exposed.

I decided it would be better to take our time, stick to the cover of the trees all the way, working around the fringe of the clearing.

But Trina was too impatient.

Before I could make my suggestion, she was stepping forward through the bushes, heading straight across the clearing.

Well, you know how it is.

Wrong move though I knew it was, I had to go along with her now, sticking close.

"Well take it easy then!" I whispered, gripping her arm. "Keep your ears open. So long as we can hear that digging, we—"

Then I froze.

So did Trina.

The digging sound had stopped!

It must only have been for a second or two that we stood frozen there like that, slap in the middle of the clearing.

But it was long enough.

Long enough for the woman to emerge from her side, give a little yelp, drop the spade and the big bunch of green stuff she was carrying, and say:

"*You*! . . . *Again*!"

We unfroze. We didn't stop to argue. Her face had that twisted popeyed look once more and she was moving forward. So we turned and we ran.

"Stop!" she yelled behind us.

We ran faster.

"Come right back here!"

Faster still.

"I will not *have* it!"

Faster, faster.

The next sound behind us was the slam of a car door.

But now we were dragging our bikes out of the hollow.

I didn't even think about the plans for escape that I'd been mulling over earlier: about how it might be better to abandon the bikes and plunge through the corn where the car couldn't follow. Right then we were back on wheels and that was all that seemed to matter.

So we began to pedal and as soon as we got going along the road between the corn and the grass, I started listening out for the car engine.

"Faster, Trina," I said. "She hasn't started it yet."

"Started—what?"

"The car. She—"

"*Hey*!"

The voice came from behind us. And not far.

My neck prickled as I wondered if this was a witch or something, who was *flying* after us.

Then I realized it hadn't been a woman's voice at all.

"Ray!" cried Trina, glancing around and going into a wobble.

It was our brother all right.

Pedalling furiously on his bike.

"Keep going, you dum-dums!" he said, catching up. "And thank your stars you've got someone in the outfit who can use his head!"

"*I'll find out where you live!*" came another voice now.

We turned again.

The woman.

"I'll track you down!"

Standing just by the trees at the bend.

"I'll see your parents!"

"Keep going," said Ray. "She can't have found the keys yet."

"What keys?" I asked, as we swerved around another bend.

"Car keys," he said. "They were in the ignition. I crept up and took them out. Before you came. Just in case something like this happened. I put them on the floor by the brake pedal. She'll find them, but not before we're clear of the place."

"You mean you've been here all afternoon?" said Trina.

I thought of the twig we'd heard.

"Sure!" said Ray. "I couldn't leave a couple of idiots like you to tangle with a cunning murderess, could I?"

"You—*you* think she is one now?" said Trina.

"Phooey!" said Ray. "When I saw her with the spade I admit I got to wondering. But then I was around that side and I saw what she was digging up."

"What?"

"Potatoes. Spinach. She has a little vegetable patch over by the creek."

I groaned.

"After all *that*!" I said, glaring at Trina. "And now she's threatening to tell Mom and Dad!"

"Yeah," said Ray. "We just have to hope she doesn't trace us before Saturday afternoon!"

17

THE FINAL CLUE

But she has found out where we live.

Oh, yes!

And so she has seen our parents.

Oh yes, indeed!

This morning. This Friday morning. The morning of our last full day.

Even before she turned up, we'd been feeling pretty gloomy.

It looked like rain again—hazy, heavy, dull.

But it wasn't that that made us feel the way we did. It wasn't even the prospect of having to ride around in wet clothes all day, seeking out trailers and trailer camps, inquiring about the cat.

It was the thought that this was the only clue we had left to work on. And it was also the feeling behind the thought that if *that* failed the cat was surely doomed.

He didn't seem to feel all this, though. Amnesia was

the only one among us around that breakfast table who seemed to have anything cheerful to look forward to. He was a bit restless, sure, but in a chipper sort of way—his green eyes bright as they looked up at us, his tail high in the air as he stalked around, rubbing against our legs and butting our shins with his forehead like a little furry bull without horns.

Maybe he knew something we didn't. *We* were so gloomy that even his behaviour didn't brighten us. If anything, it made us feel worse. Only Katie had the heart to respond, and then only by dropping a limp hand at her side to give him a stroke in passing.

Then:

"Uh-huh!" went Trina.

She had been to the stove to get some more egg and she had glanced out of the window.

I heard an engine come to a stop.

"What's wrong?" asked Mom.

"Oh, nothing!" said Trina, trying to sound unconcerned. "It's just that I think we have a visitor."

"Oh, well," said Ray, suddenly getting up from the table, "we can't hang around here all day, you guys! We have work to do."

I think he had the idea of sneaking out at the front and over the grass.

But—no way.

The driver of the car was sounding the horn.

Dad winced over his coffee.

"Why can't they come to the door?" he complained. "Making that row!"

"Maybe there's something wrong," Mom said. "Sounds rather urgent."

She went out through the summer kitchen and opened the door.

"Hi!" came a women's voice.

Hers! The Strange Lady of the Trailer.

"Look, you guys—" Ray began again.

"Be quiet!" said Dad. "I'm trying to hear what it's all about."

". . . sorry to bother you like this, but I believe you have a cat here."

That's what the woman was saying.

"Ha!" said Dad. "Looks like we have a firm inquiry after all. Come on!"

Well, he didn't know what we knew, of course.

Nobody rushed after him.

We just hung around there, knowing it was too late to escape now, and wondering what to say.

"Yes, we do have a cat," Mom was saying. "It's a stray. We've been looking all over for its owners. Don't tell me—"

"No. Not mine." The woman's voice sounded strained. I peeped out. Her face looked strained too, as she looked up at Mom from the window of the car. It was only opened part way, I noticed. "The reason I'm asking—*one* reason I'm asking—is because I have a terrible allergy to cats. I came here to recover from a bad sickness and I daren't take any chances. Is the cat shut up in the house somewhere?"

"He is now," said Dad, closing the door behind him and stepping out. "May I ask what this visit's about?"

"You may," said the woman, lowering the window full down and looking relieved, but still very tight around the mouth. "Apart from the—the animal, you do have four children here, I understand? Two boys and two girls, they told me at the Haywood farm."

"Yes. Sure. What—"

"Well will you *please* tell them to stop harrassing me?" blurted the woman, her face beginning to twitch.

"Oh, gosh!" whispered Trina. "She looks like she's going to cry!"

"Harrassing you?" Mom was saying. "But I don't understand. Our children aren't the sort—"

"But they did, they *did*! Yesterday afternoon, spying on me, after coming around in the morning and thrusting the—the cat—in my face, giving me the shock of my life!"

"Oh dear!" Mom said. "I—"

"*All right, you guys!*" Dad's voice. And Dad's face, turned to the kitchen window, eyes glinting. "*Out here! All of you! Right now!*" The woman clutched his sleeve and said something. "*Oh yes!*" he said, turning back to us. "*And make sure the cat doesn't come out with you!*"

So out we went: Ray first, Trina next, then me, then Katie.

"Yes! Those are they!" said the woman. "Oh, how could you?"

Ray swallowed.

"Ma'am," he said, "truly—we meant no harm."

"We were just inquiring," said Trina. "Honestly."

"We only wanted to find a home for the cat," I said.

"He's a lovely cat really, he won't hurt you, shall I fetch him and—?"

"*No!!*" we all roared at Katie.

"Sorry!" she said, looking scared.

"So are the rest of us sorry, too," said Ray, looking back at the woman. "We apologize, ma'am."

"Yes," I said.

"Very sincerely!" said Trina, who'd gone all red and had tears in her eyes, and looked thoroughly ashamed, as well she might, all *she'd* been saying about the woman.

"Well, I accept that," said the woman. "But *why*? Why come back to spy on me?"

We looked at one another. Or—more correctly—Ray and I looked at Trina and Katie looked at her shoes.

"Well?" said Dad, sounding grim again.

Well, all right.

How *do* you tell someone you thought they'd got a body buried in their vegetable patch?

"Er—" Trina cleared her throat. "I—we—I mean I—"

"Trina had this idea, you see." It was Ray who took over, coming to the aid of his sister. "She saw that the cat didn't know about doors that open and shut on hinges. So she figured it must have lived someplace where they only had sliding doors. And that suggested a trailer. So we came to see you. Then we noticed that your outside door *was* hinged. But Trina still said the doors inside a trailer are usually sliding and—"

"Ah! I see!" For the first time we'd known her, the woman had a smile on her face. "So you thought you'd come and check it out. Take a peek inside my trailer while I was out."

Well, if that was the explanation that made her smile, why upset her with the real one?

Trina must have been thinking the same. But she has a

conscience, that girl, as well as an imagination. One is almost as strong as the other and they both get her into whole lots of trouble. So—as she told us afterward—she was just about to correct the woman, when Dad exploded and saved her.

"But why didn't you go up to this lady properly and *ask* to see the inside? Sneaking up like that! I never thought any child of mine—"

"No! Please! Don't be hard on them." The woman was smiling again. She was really beginning to look kind of nice. "After my reaction in the morning they'd be too *scared* to ask. I bet they thought I was a madwoman. Didn't you?"

"Huh—well—"

"Well, not exactly—I mean—"

"We just kind of—"

"*I* wasn't there the second time!" piped up Katie. "I was back here, playing with the cat!"

The woman winced a bit, but still smiled on.

"Ah, yes! There's that. That's some mystery you have on your hands there, kids!"

"Yes," sighed Mom. "But I'm afraid time's running short now."

"Tell me," said the woman, looking at Trina, "what *is* this thing about sliding doors? I mean I accept what you say, of course, but just how can you tell a cat isn't used to the ordinary kind of doors?"

Trina explained. The woman looked impressed.

"Now you've got *me* intrigued," she said. "Oh well . . . I hope you get lucky. But I have to tell you, they aren't all sliding doors inside a trailer. Not in mine, anyway. The clothes closet and cupboards, yes. But—"

Then she stopped. Her eyes opened wide. "Hey! Say! Have you tried boats?"

We stared at her. I was wondering if she'd started going crazy again.

She snapped her fingers at us.

Her smile came on really wide now.

"Come on! Come on! Boats! We're near the river here, aren't we? Boats! Don't *they* have sliding doors to save space? In those small cabin cruisers they do, I'm sure."

We gaped at one another.

We'd never thought about that!

Later, Trina claimed it for her own. She said if we hadn't followed up her trailer clue we'd never have bugged the woman. And if we hadn't bugged the woman she'd never have driven around and given us the boat idea.

Ray said he'd probably have gotten around to it before long. He said it might even have occurred to him that the reason Amnesia got scared that time we lifted the table was because on boats the tables are fixed to the floor and it must have looked spooky.

But I doubt that he'd have thought of all this in time.

Anyway, it was a marvellous new clue the woman had given us.

And since it was the last full day for us to follow *any* clue up, it looked like the final clue, successful or not.

"Excuse us," said Ray. "Now we really do have work to do!"

18

THE FINAL REPORT

I made that last report yesterday, in the evening, after the longest busiest search yet: The Great Boat Search. It had to be the busiest because yesterday was our last full day and today, Saturday, would not have been much use at all, on account of the packing and locking up and having to leave here by early afternoon.

So *busy* it had to be—right from the moment the trailer lady gave us the clue—and *long* it sure turned out to be. And even at the end of it, last night, there was still a chance that it might all have been a waste of time. That is why I said nothing about the search in yesterday's report. Because *One*: I was tired; and *Two*: I was scared of blowing our good luck by being too sure of success before it was definitely certain.

OK. So back to the scene yesterday morning in the back yard, when Ray said:

"Now we really do have work to do."

"Wait!" said Dad. "Looks like you need help on this one. What do you propose to do?"

"What we've done before," said Ray. "Make inquiries at the two nearby towns. Only this time do what we *should* have done before. Take the boats into account. Concentrate on the boat-owners, ships' stores, places like that."

"Right," said Dad. "But this time you have to remember you're dealing with transients—mobile people. The boat the cat came from—if he *did* come from a boat—could be farther upriver by now. Or farther *down*river. So listen. This is what I suggest. . . ."

Well, it was a great suggestion and it put real heart into us. It meant that while we kids were working the two nearby river towns, the other river towns would not be neglected. Because why? Because not only Mom and Dad, but most *everybody* helped. Even the trailer lady. Right away, she said she'd be glad to—kidding a little when she said it, by adding:

"If only to make sure that there is one cat less in the area after today!"

So she went in her car to make inquiries farther down the river, while Dad and Mom went in our car to make inquiries farther up the river.

"And to coordinate everything and make sure we're constantly in touch and no time is wasted," said Dad, just before we all split—he and Mom in one direction, the lady in the opposite direction, and we kids in yet another—"we'll stop by at the Haywood place and ask if we can use their phone. That way we'll have someplace to call back every hour or so to give progress reports and swap information and call off the search if and when necessary."

That was another great idea. Somehow it made all the difference, when we were slogging around those two towns, to be able to pick up the phone every now and then, in the hope of better news from farther along the river.

True enough, it could have been depressing too, to hear Nibs or Sherry answer and say: "No. No news yet." Which they did, time after time. But they would also add things like:

"But your Dad's just called to say they're trying the next town up, which is more popular with boating people."

Or:

"The trailer lady's called in to say she's discovered that quite a few boats do carry cats in the crew, so we must be on the right track."

Things like that would give us new hope.

It made us feel sure that sooner or later we just *had* to turn up something strong by way of a lead. If of course there was anything to *be* turned up.

Well, there was.

And guess who lit on it first?

No. Not the trailer lady.

And not Mom and Dad.

And not even us.

It was Nibs—sitting there in the Haywood farmhouse and never moving more than three or four feet from the phone.

Now I have to tell you that Nibs was feeling just as anxious about the cat as we were. He and Sherry had grown quite fond of it during those two days it was in their attic, and the thought of it having to die made them very sad. (In fact, although he would never admit it, I think it was Nibs who had mistakenly left the door or maybe a window open that night, which made him feel worse than ever.)

So anyway, those two farm kids had not even left the phone for lunch, but had sat there munching peanut butter sandwiches, ready to snatch it up at the first ring. And the reason I know this is that one time I called in I caught Nibs with a mouthful and it was hard to make out what he was saying at first.

But that's not the point.

This is.

Here's how Nibs came to hit the jackpot just sitting there and using his knowledge of the locality.

It was late afternoon. We had covered both nearby towns and got exactly zero. In fact we'd got less than zero, a real minus, because we'd been finding out that some boats *do* have hinged doors, after all. So, what with one thing and another, we were a bit depressed at last, I have to admit, when I called in and told Nibs we were through.

"You tried *everywhere*?"

I said yes.

"Both towns?"

I said yes, yes, sure, did he think we'd be quitting already if we hadn't?

"Every boat-owner?"

"Every boat-owner we could find," I said wearily.

"And nobody knows anything?"

"No."

"Nothing at *all*?"

"Nothing."

"Not even at the Yacht Club?"

"The what?"

(It sounded like Hot Club the way Nibs said it.)

"The Yacht Club. You mean you never tried the *Yacht Club*?"

"Listen," I said. "If it's on the waterfront in either of these two towns and it has boats moored alongside, we tried it!"

Nibs nearly came marching down that phone.

"No, no, no! It isn't *in* town, you dummy! It's near it but not in it. Listen. You make a left turn just before you reach town from this side, near the Episcopalean Church. Old River Lane it's called and it brings you out at—"

I didn't wait for any more.

"I'll call you back," I said, and hung up.

At the Yacht Club we were taken to see a man called the Commodore. Big guy, with a blazer and a white cap and a red silk scarf in the neck of his shirt. I'll always remember him. He was standing at a bar, having a drink, and he listened very politely to what Trina said.

"No," he murmured. "I'm sorry. I guess if any of our members or guests had lost a cat, they would—"

"Hey, wait a minute!"

This was another man, who'd been sitting nearby.

"Did you say *cat*? A grey and black striped cat?"

I felt myself tingle all over just the way I had yesterday, but this time with hope, not fear.

We told him yes.

"That's funny," he said. "We just got in from Guilford further down the coast and there's some Australian ketch skipper turning the place inside out, looking for one of those."

"Guilford?" we all said together.

The Commodore frowned.

"That's a long way from here. I doubt if a cat would have come all—hey! Wait. You said a ketch? An *Australian* ketch?"

The other man nodded. We were jerking our heads from one man to the other like a tennis game.

"Why," said the Commodore, "that must be the Donovans. Sure. On some kind of a world cruise, the whole family. Two little girls with them. Didn't know about a cat, though. They were our guests here last week. Friday. Saturday. Yes. The storm. They left in the morning before it had quite blown over. Said they had an important date in Guilford and . . ."

Well, you can guess how we were feeling. Ray had gone dead white, Trina was laughing but with tears down her cheeks, and Katie was jumping up and down with joy.

But we still had to make sure.

The Commodore got on the phone to someone in Guilford right away. Then there was a wait while they found Mr. Donovan. Then when he came on the line, Ray had to describe the cat.

"Well it *sounds* like ours," said Mr. Donovan.

(We all had our ears pressed close to the receiver.)

"But we didn't miss him till we were in the harbour here," he said. "I suppose he *could* have slipped away back up at the Yacht Club there, what with the storm and the hurry we were in. But still . . . There are lots of them, you know—grey and black tabbies."

"Give me the phone," I said.

Then I gave Mr. Donovan the full description, the one

that I had on tape, right down to the crack in his head and the black speck on his pink nose, and that did it.

"That sounds like our cat all right," said Mr. Donovan. "He did get a bad crack on the skull—a glancing blow from the wheel of a truck while we were berthed in Cape Town last year. And the black speck fits. Yes. Well, it's certainly worth our going back up there to make sure. The girls have been brokenhearted over this. Look, son, put me on to the Commodore, will you?"

So I did and Mr. Donovan made arrangements to be there the following morning, which is this morning, and then the Commodore put him on to Ray again, and they arranged a ten A.M. meeting, at the Yacht Club, with the cat.

Well, I'll keep you in suspense no longer.

That meeting has taken place.

We were all there, except the trailer lady, who excused herself and hoped we'd understand.

There was Mom and Dad, us Bleeker kids, Mrs. Haywood, and Nibs and Sherry, and of course the cat.

On the other side, there was Mr. Donovan, who is very tall and thin and tanned, Mrs. Donovan, and two little girls, twins, a bit younger than Katie, called Patricia and Judy.

The meeting took place on the deck of the Emu III, which is one great boat I will tell you, and at first everyone on both sides looked very uptight as Trina and Katie set the duffel bag down.

But then, when they opened the zipper, and the cat blinked and looked around, all the Donovans went mad.

"It is! It is!" yelled the two little girls.

"Thank the Lord!" said Mrs. Donovan.

"And thank these kids!" said Mr. Donovan.

"That's OK," said Ray, on behalf of us all.

"Our pleasure," said Trina.

"I wish he was coming with *us*!" moaned Katie.

To tell the truth, we others felt a touch sad, too.

As for the cat, well, you know what he did?

He just stood there, half in the bag, half out, and looked around, and cussed.

He did. I'm sure. He just *yelled* at those Donovans, as if to say:

"You dum-dums, for going without me like that!"

But he soon got over it when the little girls picked him up and started loving him.

So what now?

Well, I'll tell you.

Maybe you've been hearing something in the background. Seagull noises. Water noises. Chugging noises. Sometimes a cat noise—a happy one this time.

That is because I am making my report on the deck of the Emu III, shipmates!

The cat has been playing with Katie and Trina and Sherry and Patricia and Judy—frisking like a kitten, showing off, climbing ropes, that sort of thing—but now he is all peaceful near me, lying on the boards and looking through the rail at the waves the way he used to look at the grass from the porch.

Ray and Nibs have been in the wheelhouse, talking to Mr. Donovan and learning how to navigate.

Nibs and Sherry will be getting off at New Haven, where Mr. and Mrs. Haywood are driving down to meet them later today—the boat trip being the farm kids' reward for all the help they gave us.

But us Bleeker kids—wowee!—you know what our reward is?

A trip all the way to Philadelphia by boat.

Yes, sir!

Instead of going back with Mom and Dad by car, we've been allowed to accept the Donovans' invitation, and the next time we see Philly will be in about a week, from the deck of the Emu III, as we sail up the Delaware.

"It'll help the cat to settle," said Mrs. Donovan.

"It'll help Katie to get used to being without it," said our Mom.

"By the way, what *is* its name?" said Dad.

Then the Donovans told us.

"Ebenezer!"

"So *that*'s why he pricked up his ears at the word 'amnesia'!" said Ray.

"Look, he's done it again this time!" said Patricia.

"Oh, let's call him that instead!" said Judy.

So they have started to do that, and I must say, judging from the way he just heaved a deep satisfied sigh at the sound of it when I said it, he seems to enjoy being a cat called Amnesia.